Obsidian Liquor
Copyright 2014 Scarlett Dawn

Cover Design by
Formatting by R.A. Mizer of ShoutLines.
For more information visit Shoutlinesdesign.com.

Cover photography by SC Photo
http://www.scphotoaz.com/

Cover Model Tommy Barresi
https://www.facebook.com/tommy.beressi

OBSIDIAN LIQUOR

SCARLETT DAWN

DEDICATION

CHAPTER 1

November 1, 2014
The first day of the charity event…

I knew I was having a rotten day when not only did my rental car break down, but the tow truck hauling my decrepit rental also broke down—when I was already late for work to begin with.

With smoke billowing from under the popped hood of the tow truck, I cursed quietly at the man bending over the engine. I did not have time for this. Not today.

I glanced down the deserted road lined with exotic trees. "How far until Palm Resort?"

The guy's dirt smeared face lifted. He glanced around and scratched his head with the screwdriver—*what the hell was he going to do with that*—and pointed in the direction I already knew I needed to go. "That way. About three miles."

I sighed and wiped the sweat from my forehead. It was fucking hot in Key West. "Look, I'm going to walk it." I pulled out my business card and belatedly realized my own hands were just as dirty as his were from when I had attempted to fix the rental myself. "My name's Elizabeth Forter. This is my cell number. Have the rental service call me when they have a replacement ready."

Nodding, he took the card. "Will do, Ms. Forter. I'm sorry about the inconvenience."

Not replying to that comment, I turned and started walking. Maybe I would write a piece on their crappy service. It would serve them right. I was missing a possibly big story. I felt it in my gut. I did not care what the rags in Moscow said. I knew deep down that Grigori Kozar and Ember Lerrus were an item, even if the past two months had been dead in the water with Ember seen on dates with Cole Donovan and Brent Terrance, and Grigori being seen with a new player from Russia, Zoya Petrova.

There was just something there. Moreover, all of them were hot news.

Anyone who got any scoop where Brent and Cole were concerned was going to make the front page since news of their return from a massively successful military mission had spread like wildfire. In addition, I had a 'thing' for the Donovans and their money. The Mayor, Cole's father, had shut down so many of my stories that I felt a sense of true triumph every time I was able to splash Cole's name in an unbecoming way. So I was here to dig dirt up on the Donovans via Grigori and Ember. Brent, Cole, and Ember were supposedly in a serious relationship, old news from a month ago stating they were a threesome, and if I could prove that Ember was stepping out on them, it would make Cole look like a real schmuck.

I snickered and quickened my pace, but my short legs could only go so fast. A mile down the road—*thank you road marker*—I started regretting my heels. Not to mention, my huge bag I was rolling behind me.

How much shit had I packed?

Did I really need that extra Prada purse? Or my forth pair of black heels? Hmm…yes.

Yes, I did. My hard-earned paychecks helped me look good.

By the time I arrived at the resort, I was wearing sweat-soaked silk that clung to my body that was decorated with dust and smears of oil where I had wiped my hands to sign the check-in forms. I breathed in the cool air, and asked the long nosed man behind the counter, "How long until the Brick Foundation Event starts?"

He checked the resort's schedule and glanced at the clock. "You're press?" When I nodded, he stated, "You have a half hour before they allow the press inside."

I glanced to the enormous interior of the resort, knowing I would never make it. "Do you have a map of this place?" He did. He even circled the building I needed to go to, where my room was, and where I currently was. "Thank you so much."

"You're welcome, Ms. Forter. Enjoy your stay," he

3

replied politely, handing over my room card before motioning for the next person in line to step forward.

I studied the map, extremely confused until I realized it was upside down.

I flipped the stupid thing right side up.

That was better.

I dashed to my room, and took the quickest shower possible. I threw on my staid tan skirt suit, pairing it with a pink camisole that was light and airy. I did not have time to dry my hair, so I ran a wide-spaced comb through my short riot of strawberry blonde curls and added mousse so it did not frizz too badly in the humidity here. A little lip-gloss, some mascara, my silver thin glasses, my press badge, my purse, and I was ready to rock.

At the last minute, I grabbed my duffle that was full of cameras, tape recorders, and video equipment from one of the packages that had already been delivered to my room this morning before my arrival. God, I loved a praiseworthy resort.

This job had originally been given to a newbie, but I had pestered my editor enough that he had allowed me to take the assignment. However, I was flying solo. I had been given the same resources that the newbie would have been allotted. I had splurged a bit of my own money on items that I had researched online before coming here. A little undercover work was going to be needed.

I made it to the building that was as big as an arena just as the other press members were arriving. I did not recognize any of them because they were all lower on the totem pole than I in the news business; however, I quickly shot photos of all of them with my camera phone before they noticed me. I may be plain and young, but my face was now known to the news world, thanks to when I uncovered Jake Donnally was really Grigori Kozar, the son of Daniil Kozar, the head of the Russia mafia.

Sometimes, my accolades were a plus.

Most days, they were a real hindrance.

I knew as soon as the other press members noticed me. They started whispering and covertly watching me where I stood in the back of the group while waiting for Mrs. Donovan to give her speech. After she was through speaking, we would be allowed inside and down on the main floor. I had not done this kind of work in so long, I was actually a little nervous.

I hoped it was like riding a bike.

Mrs. Donovan stepped outside the doors where I could hear many rowdy voices and shouts. She looked as beautiful as ever, even dressed down in dress slacks and a simple silk shirt. Her black hair was loose today around her tan face, and her dark brown eyes gleamed as she warmly smiled at all of us. "Hello, everyone. Thank you so much for coming." I quickly turned on my tape recorder and lifted it high, since I was in the back. "First, I want to welcome you. This event is supporting Brick Foundation, a charity that strives to give education to those less fortunate in Africa. It will be a two-week event. You will receive the itinerary as you walk through the doors. There will be many celebrities and politicians coming that the firefighters, police, armed forces, and security individuals inside have helped at some time in their lives. There are many events planned and they're all over this resort, so please pay attention to your itineraries or you may miss out on an event."

Her smile brightened even further. "This is a new charity and they need your support in making their name known, so please make sure to include their name in your pieces, and not just who is kissing whom and who's wearing what." We all chuckled...because that was partially the truth. "I hope you enjoy the festivities and donate if you are able. The first event starts in two hours. The public will be allowed inside in an hour, so feel free to do your interviews until then. However, be careful. These are trained individuals, but they are warming up for the competition. I wouldn't want you to get hurt." She opened the steel double doors, and motioned for us to go inside.

I clicked off my tape recorder and darted into the fold. My name had only just today been changed on the press list so they could not blackball me at the last minute, and I did not want to be seen before I could get in. Once I was in, it was cake. They could not throw a fit if I was already inside. As long as they did not catch me doing anything wrong, anyway.

I grabbed an itinerary as they were handed out and pushed through the crowd walking between the bleachers. The room was only part of the building from the size of it. It appeared like a boxing arena with bleachers on all four walls, and a literal boxing ring in the middle. The bleachers were not fully extended yet, so there were groups all over the place warming up in sweatpants, gi pants, or sports bras and shorts. My gaze swung across the space until I quickly spotted my prey. They were in a large group in the corner across the room.

I scrutinized the layout for access. Hidden access.

I did not want to be seen just yet.

It was not hard to perceive my only option, the bleachers.

I moved with a group of press that was heading to the opposite corner, but along the same wall as my target. They asked questions and I politely answered them, seeing the same look of awe on their faces that tended to drive me crazy. Someone tapped my shoulder, and I glanced back...and slammed right against someone.

"Oh, shit. I'm sorry," I mumbled as the smell of roses invaded my senses. I hurried to straighten my glasses and peered way, way up. I dropped my head just as quickly. I promptly maneuvered out of the hold that Grigori's father, Daniil, the man I had slammed into, had on me, trying to keep me steady. Stupidly, I repeated myself. "Sorry."

I had no clue if he even knew what I looked like, but I had seen him plenty.

He moved aside easily enough, allowing me to catch up with my group.

OBSIDIAN LIQUOR

The man that had tapped my shoulder was chuckling. "You better pay attention to what Mrs. Donovan said. Some of those people look like they could crush me, much less someone as small as you."

I nodded—*duh*—and slipped through their group to the front edge.

As soon as they landed in the corner right where I wanted, I stepped back, surveying everyone. No one was watching me, so I ducked under the bleacher that was only out a few steps. I progressed through the darkness slowly, going straight, the only way I could, right toward my target.

I stopped a few feet back and stayed in the shadows.

Ember was stretching her calves against the wall and talking to a fine-looking guy. I mentally ran through the list of names I knew…Lev something or other. I pulled out my tape recorder and whispered the date and time, along with Ember's and Lev's names, and held the device closer to them, listening.

"I'm telling you, I bet I beat your time. It'll be a fair wager. We have no clue who we're going to be fighting," Lev stated, stretching his hamstrings.

Ember stared with cold eyes and shrugged. "Whatever. I just want to get in the ring with someone talented. But I'll take the bet. What did you say? A grand?"

Lev nodded. "A grand." He eyed her as she went back to gazing at the wall and switching feet. He asked

8

softly, "Ember, is everything all right? You seem a little…distant."

"I'm fine," she muttered quickly, hugging the wall to get a good stretch.

"It's been a while since we talked. We could have a drink after this and catch up."

"I don't think Brent and Cole would like that." Her head fell against the wall, pushing harder. "Maybe when things calm down some. They've only been back a month."

Lev reached out and gripped her chin, turning her face toward him. He studied her, and asked bluntly, "Are you happy with them? Still happy? They were gone for two years."

Her gaze went even more frigid. She stayed silent for a long few moments before she finally spoke. "We're getting to know each other again. Time will tell."

He dropped his hand. "Well, I'm here if you really want to talk."

Ember smiled, kind of, as she stepped back from the wall. "Thanks." She spun away and strolled to Zane Harris, one of the owners of their company, Lion Security, who was standing in the corner talking with Cole.

Eva Kozar, another one of the mafia brats, moved next to Lev, so I yanked the recorder back, ready to state her name…but I stalled when I felt unusual heat behind me.

I clicked the recorder off, stuffed it down my bra, and swiftly turned. It was hard to see in the darkness, but I pushed my glasses up and stared at the man that had come up behind me. It was Roman Kozar; seriously, they had a lot of damn siblings. He silently stared down at me before glancing behind me, taking in what I had almost gotten on tape. My heart was pounding in my ears, and I was more than freaked when he still did not say anything, only grabbed my arm and manhandled me out the way I had come, thankfully not the end that would take me right into their group.

I quickly saw why he went this way when he none-to-gently tossed me out from behind the stands. Daniil, his bodyguards, Artur Kozar—another mafia kid—and Stash Bailey, a co-owner of Lion Security, were all standing there. A pretty damn formidable group. I was not afraid to say that I was a little intimidated by all their bulging muscles and testosterone, but I kept my mouth shut. There was no need to start babbling what I had been doing, and plus, I had no clue how long Roman had been standing behind me.

Daniil glanced at Roman, raising his eyebrows.

Roman quietly spoke in Russian.

I bit my cheek in frustration. I had no clue what the hell he was saying.

Daniil peered at me. His stare was a warning. "What were you doing, Ms. Forter?"

So he did know who I was. The jerk had probably followed me after I had bumped him.

I shrugged and went with the semi-truth. "Getting a story."

"What story might that be?" Stash asked, his gaze roaming me in an assessing way. We had never met before, so this was my first up close and personal with the man.

I shrugged again. "Brent and Cole are big news. Anything that I can put in print that others don't have is good business." Sticking to the truth as much as possible was always key when caught snooping. And I was press. They expected it of me.

"Hear anything interesting?" Daniil asked gently.

Instinct had me taking a step back. The man was chilling on a different level. "Nothing I didn't already know." Ember was not happy with Brent and Cole. She always smiled pretty for the cameras, but her eyes gave her away. Anyone who hid that much in her gaze was not happy.

"What a shame," Daniil stated slowly. He glanced at Artur, speaking in Russian before his regard returned to me. "Artur will be your escort while you interview the group you were spying on." He bent, and I froze like a skittish deer as he placed his mouth against my ear, my damp hair being pressed against my head. "If I ever catch you spying on any of my children, you will never write another article. Because you won't have hands to do it with."

I started trembling at the blatant honesty in his tone as he leaned back and smiled charmingly. Right before he angled his body differently, and with reflexes I sure as hell did not have, he slipped his hand down my camisole right into my bra. My eyes widened as he grabbed the tape recorder and pulled in out just as swiftly as he had stuck his hand down my top.

My reflex came naturally to any man that would have done that.

I smacked him across his face. I was smart enough to realize that was a really bad move, and stumbled back just as quickly, slamming against the bleachers.

Silence extended as he slowly straightened, his gaze wandering over me, his expression one of disdain as he rubbed his cheek. He did not even need to say anything. His look said it all. I was not his type. Never would be. I was beneath him.

My eyes narrowed. But I did not say anything. I had just poked the shark with…not even a sharp stick…more like, a twig. It was just enough to irritate him and make him notice me. I sure as hell did not want to be his dinner.

Then, he opened his big fat mouth. "You shouldn't hide something like this in an area so small. It's too noticeable." He twirled the tape recorder between his fingers, his lips twitching as he started to turn to walk away.

My eyes narrowed even further and I crossed my arms over my B-cups, more than a little self-conscious. "I'm sure you know plenty about small things, old man. I hear with age appendages tend to shrivel." I let my lips twitch as his had. "Like prunes."

Stash choked.

Roman snorted.

I quickly backed away as Daniil turned in my direction, utterly honed on my face.

Luckily, Stash and Roman intercepted him and herded him away.

Artur was staring with stunned amusement. "You really don't want to piss him off." He jerked his head at his dad. "And you just did."

I shrugged, staring at the tape recorder Daniil was pocketing. I had more, and an excellent memory, but still, that would be coming out of my paycheck. Not to mention, I knew Artur was right. I had possibly just started something that I was in no way prepared for.

Sounding bored, when he did not get a comment from me, Artur asked, "Do you want an interview with my group, or not?"

"Might as well," I muttered, knowing I needed to give something to my editor tonight.

Artur escorted me to Lion Security's group.

I interviewed each one, receiving only curt answers even when I kept the questions acceptable to the event. Though playing the good little reporter for the charity, my cover was most definitely blown.

Brick Foundation's event was set up with different categories. Lone sparring, gun control, group defense, group offense, partner sparring, partner sparring for show, weapons show, and an obstacle course, group and loner. There was not enough time for all of them to be done in one day, so each event had been split up for different days and times, only three hours in the morning, and three hours in the evening.

There were no rules for men against women, supposedly they were all trained enough to fight any weight group or sex. At the end of the two weeks, they would tally what groups had the most wins. The top two teams would then pick which person/persons they wanted to compete in each event again for a grand finale. During the evenings, every third night, there were parties planned.

Tonight was lone sparring. As the celebrities entered, I snapped photos of them in their casual attire as they were given score cards, where they were to mark down how much they would like to donate based on each match. I was sure they already had a total amount they wanted to give, but this allowed them to play-act making bets. In the end, no one lost any money. They had given it to charity and gotten to see their favorite 'life saver' in action. Really, for a Donovan planned event, it was damn genius.

Once the lights started blinking, indicating the event was about to begin, Mrs. Donovan and her husband, the Mayor, slipped into the ring. A mike was lowered, just like in a real boxing match, and polite applause ensued. I quickly took my seat in the chairs provided on one side for the press that were barely squeezed between a fully extended bleacher and the ring. I was right up front, and loving it. I had grabbed a seat smack in the middle on the front row right when the bleachers were pulled out. I guess I had not lost my touch for the newbie stuff.

I flicked my other tape recorder on, while I dug in my duffle for my high-zoom camera. I quickly snapped a photo of the Mayor and Mrs. Donovan as they said a few words that explained the events and where the proceeds of the donations would go.

A referee stepped into the ring as the competing groups entered from a side door, their assigned sitting area directly behind the press on one-half of the bleachers. I scanned the groups entering and started laughing quietly when I saw my target group. They were wearing hot pink tank tops or sports bras with black athletic shorts. There were not many women at Lion Security, and it looked damn funny seeing them in that color. By their expressions, they were not entirely too pleased with it either.

I zeroed in on Cole, Brent, Grigori, and Ember, snapping many shots. Oddly, Ember was wearing a tank top like the men, instead of a sports bra like the women of their group. She was a Goth girl, but I had not expected her to be bashful. I pulled out my notepad, and quickly wrote that information down to investigate later.

Up in the boxing ring, the referee was filling the bejeweled top hat that Mrs. Donovan handed him with different colors of paper, the colors of the competitor's team shirts that had a participant's name on each slip. If Mrs. Donovan drew the same color in a row, she would then put the second slip back and keep drawing until she drew one of a different color.

That was how the competitors were to be picked.

Forget clever technology, they were drawing out of a hat.

A sparkly one at that...in a savage competition of America's finest.

If that was not a great reason to dislike the Donovans...well, I had a hundred others.

Once the competing groups were seated, Mrs. Donovan reached into the hat. I had already finished writing down which groups corresponded to the colors by one of the programs I had snatched. She drew a lime green slip first. Titus Protection. She stated the name of the individual, and a brute of a man made his way through the stands. There was polite applause, but there were also loud whistles, probably the celebrities he had previously helped. Mrs. Donovan reached into the hat again, while the Mayor quickly punched into a handheld computer, reading the participant's stats and accomplishments to the crowd. Mrs. Donovan pulled out a hot pink paper.

The Mayor glanced over her shoulder when he saw the color, and they both stared at the name a moment before glancing at the brute. Mrs. Donovan cleared her throat, her face void of any emotion, and stated clearly, "Anna Tran of Lion Security."

I blinked, trying to place a face with the name,

but she had not been in the group while I had interviewed them earlier. As applause sounded much louder than the first guys' had—not surprising since Lion Security was the top security company in the United States—I turned and zoomed my camera on their group, and stared through the lens.

Good God. That man was going to crush her.

She was not tiny like me, but she was not a fierce, muscular woman either. And honestly, she was looking a little nervous as she walked down the stairs toward the ring. That guy might be big, but it was obvious that he was fast. This was a no holds bar competition. Other than killing blows and permanent damage hits, anything went.

I turned my camera on Carl Tran of Lion Security, her husband. Oh, my goodness. He appeared like he wanted to wrap her in his arms and throw her back on her seat so he could beat the shit out of the man that was about to fight his wife. Well, this should be interesting.

I lowered my camera and quickly jotted down their names and companies. I was going to keep a tally, so I could report the match numbers accurately.

The Mayor read off her stats and accomplishments, and I was startled to realize she was the one to uncover Brent and Cole were still alive, and aided them back to the United States after their military mission was complete. Definitely a smart cookie. Still, she was damn jumpy; by the way, she kept clenching her fists.

OBSIDIAN LIQUOR

The Mayor and Mrs. Donovan left the ring while the referee stayed, explaining the rules to the competitors, even though they already knew them. If they made it through three songs without a knockout or a ten second down rule, then they would each have the opportunity to pick someone from their group to fight with them, two-on-two style. Poor Anna reminded me of a nail about to battle a house as she stood in front of her opponent.

I heard…yes…Ember shout, "Kick his weak legs, Anna!" Odd advice. Normally, it would be 'kick his ass', but whatever. It got a resounding roar from the audience.

Anna glanced back to her group, and I could have sworn she mouthed, 'Thank you'.

A ding sounded, and then rock hard music started blaring over the sound system.

Anna immediately ducked a fist that flew at her head, the blow barely missing her since the guy was fast like I had noticed. This back and forth volley went on far longer than I had imagined it would with her smaller stature. Then the guy got a glancing blow against her jaw, and she fell. But, as she did, she twisted, letting her whole body rotate with the motion, swiping behind his knees with both of hers.

The brute went down hard on his back, and they were both immediately rolling away and popping back up. Anna shook her head hard, and it was on again. I cheered right along with everyone else, trying to get decent shots when I could.

I got it when she twirled and dove at his legs when he aimed high with a fist. Again, he went down hard, but Anna went with him with a knee straight to his crotch and an elbow to his head. I snapped a picture as she did the combo. She jumped up as he rolled onto his side, one hand on his masculine bits, the other on his head. I knew the men had to be wearing some kind of cup, but she had probably broken the damn thing with how hard she had nailed him.

He did not get up. Lion Security had their first win.

An hour passed before another hot pink slip was pulled. The Mayor once again glanced over his wife's shoulder. They both blinked before Mrs. Donovan grabbed the mike, her expression actually cracking this time with worry. "Ember Lerrus from Lion Security."

The normal stats were given while I snapped photos. However, once Ember entered the ring, I focused my lens on Grigori and kept it there. This was what I was here for.

He sat stiffly with his eyes just as cold as hers.

I heard Mrs. Donovan state, "Woody Chin from the Marine Corps."

I immediately started snapping pictures as his gaze darted over the competing groups. I could not see why he stopped moving his head, but his eyes narrowed. I got pictures as his gaze altered from ice cold to fevered intensity.

His jaw clenched before he blanked the expression.

Yep. More there than meets the eye.

I lowered my camera and almost dropped it. I had not noticed before, but Daniil was seated with Zoya and his bodyguards only a few rows up on the other half of the bleachers reserved for family. He was staring right at me. I turned on my chair quickly and got my first view of Woody Chin.

Oh.

If Grigori had been sizing him up, I understood the hostility. Woody Chin was a man of Asian ancestry, tall and lean, not bulky, and the way he moved into the ring spoke of long time training. The Marines must have taught him to be an assassin with the deadly mien he wore.

Ember and I were pretty much the same size. I think I had an inch, maybe, on her, but we were both damn close to the too-tiny rage. She observed her opponent with a…creepy…gaze, and I quickly snapped a few photos before putting the camera down as she watched him move, her eyes repeatedly surveying his frame. She closed her eyes and scrubbed her face as the referee said the rules all over again. When she opened them, she glanced up to her group. I could not read what she was telling them with her expression, but her ponytail shook the slightest bit, as if she was indicating she could not beat the guy.

I could have told her that. She was going to go down. Hard.

The bell dinged and a different set of songs started. The fight was on.

Holy shit, I stared in shock as Ember held her own against this martial arts three-time black belt. They went around the ring, sometimes missing, and every so often hitting their target; effectively, kicking each other's asses.

At one point during the second song, Ember landed a solid kick to one of the man's kneecaps, but he had already started swinging his opposite leg up and hit her square in one of her shoulders. Ember gasped, her face turning white. She immediately grabbed her shoulder as they both went down. Painfully, they crawled away from one another. The place was silent as they picked themselves up. Ember did not move her hurt arm from her side, and she still managed to make it through to the last of the third song.

They stood panting and holding areas of themselves that were injured as Mrs. Donovan and the Mayor maneuvered back into the ring. Both went immediately to Ember, and the Mayor touched her shoulder. Again, her face drained to white, but she jerked back and shook her head, eyeing her competitor. He grinned even as he sucked air, favoring his knee she had knocked hard.

Mrs. Donovan raised her eyebrows in silent question.

Ember shook her head.

She sighed and grabbed the lowered mike. "Ladies and gentlemen, we have our first Death Zone match." She nodded to Woody. "You had the most blows according to the score card. You pick your teammate first."

Grinning at Ember, he stated, "My twin. Stone Chin."

Ember's eyebrows furrowed, more than likely, imaging another just like him.

He was. Stone and Woody were identical twins.

I seriously hoped those were nicknames.

As Stone got into the ring, Ember's eyes went all freaky-creepy again. So much so, that she missed Mrs. Donovan asking her whom she wanted from her team. The referee touched her shoulder, and that woke her up. She winced and pulled back, scrubbing her face again before staring up at her group.

"Ember?" Mrs. Donovan asked. "Who would you like to fight with you?"

Ember's face went cold, and she glanced back down to the men in the ring, and then back up to her group. She stated simply, "Grigori."

Instantly, I turned and started taking shots, but dammit, I had missed Grigori's initial reaction. So I altered my view to where Brent and Cole sat next to each other. It appeared Ember was going to have some explaining to do by how pissed they were, glaring at Grigori as he made his way down the bleachers.

Sorry boys, but you were gone for two years.

I made sure to keep my line of vision away from Daniil when I lowered my camera and turned back to the ring as Grigori slipped through the ropes. My gut feelings were never wrong, and Grigori had taken a position at Lion Security, the company that Ember co-owned, and kept the job, even after I had ousted him a year ago as Daniil Kozar's son.

The Mayor spoke quietly to him in passing that made Grigori's eyebrows rise, but he nodded, even as he stalked straight toward Ember. He did not pay attention to his competitors that were eyeballing him, or acknowledge that Mrs. Donovan was introducing him, or even glance up as the crowd went wild when they realized it was 'The Grigori'. He did not say anything to Ember or vice versa, but his large hands went directly to her injured shoulder.

She grimaced, turning her face from him.

I had started snapping pictures and was rewarded with a beautiful shot when he jerked her chin back around so they were face to face.

He was furious; his eyes no longer blank. She acted just as livid, but she quickly murmured to him just as the referee started reading off the rules, which effectively were, the fight continued until both teammates were down. No time limit.

Grigori's nostrils flared. He gripped her shoulder in an odd way right before he jerked his hands and a horrible snap sounded. Her complexion turned lily white, and she looked as if she wanted to puke, but Grigori briskly began massaging her shoulder. A few silent seconds passed while he worked her shoulder.

Ember's coloring sluggishly returned before she stepped away from his touch. She started wind milling her arm, a look of relief passing over her features as she rotated it faster.

And I got it all on film, baby. Grigori had just popped her shoulder back into place.

The referee was staring wide-eyed.

Ember glanced at him. "Let's do this thing." That brought on hollers from the crowd.

As the bell sounded and music blared, she and Grigori moved next to each other.

If I had thought Ember alone was spectacular, well, she and Grigori were like moving extensions of one another. Even compared to the martial arts twins that had probably been doing this since they were babies together, Ember and Grigori were breathtaking.

I stopped taking pictures just to stare.

I knew I should have had one stunning part on film; but…yeah, no, I had to watch.

Grigori spun, ducked low and kicked Woody in his injured leg, just as Ember jumped high, pressed off Grigori's back, using him like a spring, and kicked Stone straight in his jaw.

The twins did not go down from that move, but by the time the first song ended, the two men were knocked out when Ember dropped and twisted, taking both their legs out, and Grigori followed her down with two fists to the falling men's heads, knocking them unconscious before they even hit the floor. In mid-fall, Grigori rotated and landed side-by-side with Ember, both gazing at the ceiling and panting for only heartbeat before they did one of those legs to their chests, pushing back with their arms, and flipping up to their feet moves…to stand sucking air and wearing ice-cold expressions as they stared down at the fallen twins.

I could not wait any longer. I stopped gawking and brought the camera up, snapping pictures of them, all cold and deadly as sin. There was shocked silence as the music abruptly cut off, but almost immediately, an uproar of applause startled the shit out of me. Guess the fans enjoyed the show as much as I had.

Mrs. Donovan and the Mayor hopped into the ring, patting Grigori and Ember's backs while they stood as if they were dead to the world and their surroundings. It was remarkable. It made me want to dig even deeper to see what they were hiding. They could not be that way unless they were sociopaths, and I knew this was not the case because I had observed them before Brent and Cole's return.

Speaking of which, I turned my camera and zoomed in. Brent and Cole were staring with astonishment at the ring. Apparently, they were not seeing what I was. All they expressed was that they had just witnessed their girlfriend act like death's own blade, and it had shocked them. That was all.

Goody for me.

CHAPTER 2

I was attending the party that was held that night in the main ballroom of the resort. I think there was going to be more in here throughout the two weeks, but this was the first. More than likely, only the last party would be more extravagant than this one.

I was dressed in a black cocktail dress that was simple and elegant. I looked decent in it, but my hair could not be helped. I had a mass of strawberry blonde curls that the humidity was taking delight in torturing. It was like a poodle-gone-wrong hairdo. I really hated the tropics. Give me New York's blistering cold any day over this repressive humidity.

I was smart enough to make sure I brought my duffle of goods with me tonight. I did not plan to let it out of my sight. Daniil had been watching me anytime I snapped a picture anywhere near his family. The Russian mafia king would have someone try to steal it, but I was already trying to strategize a game plan for that situation. Too bad, nothing was coming to mind on that account.

Deciding to use my previous invite with Artur, I stayed close to him. The individuals here would eventually start talking as more drinks were served and lips became loose. Artur's amusement was evident when I stuck close to his side, but he let me tag along without complaint. That should have been my first clue that something was not right. However, sadly and stupidly, it was an hour into the party until I realized the asshole was staying away from the four people I wanted to be around.

I sighed, and asked bluntly, "Are you even going to go near them?"

Artur smirked. "Took you long enough to figure it out."

I crossed my arms. "Either you go over there, or I'll find a way without you."

He patted my hair. It instantly sprung back up, and he chuckled. "Natural redhead?"

"It's strawberry blonde," I muttered grumpily, swatting his hand away when he went to touch it again like a little kid. "And, yes."

He grinned but jerked his head toward Grigori, Daniil, and Zoya. "I'll take you to them."

I pointed at him. "We'll stay there for as long as I wish."

"You're awfully demanding to someone who's doing you a favor."

"You aren't doing me any favors. You're just

under daddy's orders." I smirked when he scowled. "Do you always do what daddy says?" God, I loved being a bitch sometimes.

His face hardened. "Do you want to go over there, or not?"

I nodded. "Of course."

"Then shut up and I'll take you." He muttered under his breath, but I did not catch his words as he began herding me. When we arrived, he spoke harshly to Daniil in Russian, and I swear; Grigori chuckled before he stopped himself, staring down at me.

Much like the king land shark was doing.

I waved, ignoring their hostility. "Hello." I zeroed in on Grigori, and stated softly, just loud enough to be heard over the band that was playing in the corner, "That was amazing what you and Ember did together." I paused, gauging his reaction. Which was nothing. "The logical choice would have been for her to pick Brent or Cole. You know, not to piss her men off. But she picked you. Why do you think she did that?"

Again, no reaction. Only that cold stare. "Is this on or off the record?"

I paused, really thinking. This piece about their fighting together could be a real beauty; but, in the end, I was after a different fish altogether, so I answered, "Off the record."

He shrugged. "Because she wanted to win. She knew we could do it together."

I felt my lips purse. There had to be more to it

than that. "Why would she think you would help her win where Brent or Cole couldn't?"

His own mouth twitched, and almost, dammit, almost his gaze started to crack, but I did not understand what I saw there before it was quickly blanked. "Because we practiced together for years compared to Brent, Cole, and her."

"Do you still practice together?"

"No."

"Why?" It was blunt, but an honest question. If they had been training together for years, I did not understand why they would stop now.

He placed a hand on Zoya's back and shrugged. "She's busy. I'm busy."

I decided to continue being blunt, pointing at Zoya. "Are you two an item?"

He froze for only a moment, just long enough for me to notice.

Zoya placed a hand on his chest, saying softly, "We're old friends, but we have gone on a few dates recently."

I nodded, and felt a little evil when I saw Ember, Cole, and Brent moving behind them. I pulled out my camera. "I promise not to bother you two again tonight, if you'll do me a favor." Most people wanted the press gone and far away from them. This time was not any different by their expressions.

Grigori's eyebrows rose in curiosity.

I stated, "No one has been able to get a photo of you two kissing. If I can get one, it would make my night." I shrugged when Grigori's eyebrows lifted further. "I exposed you for who you really are, so why not keep with the same reporter for this?" I smiled sweetly.

Daniil had started to crowd my personal space, but peculiarly, he moved back as I spoke, letting me have my fun. However, I stayed focused on Grigori, who was looking unwaveringly emotionless.

Zoya shrugged. "Why not? Our first kiss is on film. I wouldn't mind having a copy of it."

Ah. First kiss. I tried not to grin at that information. *Drink up, baby, drink up.*

Grigori peered at her, obviously hearing the honesty in her tone, his gaze on hers.

I quickly put the camera up to my eye, making sure to get Ember in the shot behind them. She was staring as Brent and Cole talked to Zane, silently watching as Grigori lowered his head. I immediately started hitting the fast action button, taking a least twenty shots as his lips gently touched hers, kissing her softly. Ember, her face turned whiter than when Grigori had popped her shoulder back into place...but her eyes were like a violent burning furnace she was so enraged.

God, it was a beautiful shot.

Grigori did not take the kiss too far, even when Zoya acted like she wanted to.

I lowered my camera, doing a stellar job of keeping the smirk off my face. "That was perfect. Thank you." I glanced behind them where Ember was barely keeping it together. "If you'll excuse me, I see someone else I would like to speak with. Have a nice evening."

Grigori nodded, and I started maneuvering between him and his father, but I paused, glancing back up, asking, "Out of curiosity, what did the Mayor say to you when you entered the ring with Ember?"

"Off the record?"

"Yes."

Grigori leaned down, appearing so much like his father I froze as he whispered against my ear, "That if I didn't take the bastard down, he was going to do it himself."

I blinked in astonishment. It appeared the Mayor actually had a heart, even if I did not condone violence as the means to end a problem.

Nothing else of interest happened at the ball, and I still did not know what the hell to do about the fact I would most certainly have items stolen if I went back to my room tonight. My plan was to rent another room at the resort, but I was being followed. I was certain he was one of Daniil's bodyguards that normally hovered around him. The rental car establishment still had not called with a replacement yet, so I could not leave without causing attention with a taxi to find a room elsewhere.

I was stuck until I figured out what the hell to do.

I meandered for a while until I made it to the lobby. There was a bar in one corner, and a drink was sounding swell at this point. The place had internet access so I could download my shots and work on my article that was due to my editor. Glancing behind me as I entered, I saw my tail stop and lean against a wall. He was blatantly staring now, not trying to hide the fact that he was following me.

Wonderful. When they stopped hiding, you knew you were done for.

A drink was sounding better and better.

He could not do anything to me in public, but I still needed to pick a spot that was not out in the open so I could write in peace. I was one of those people that needed absolute quiet to get the juices flowing. Same with reading a book. I just could not concentrate, and really be inventive, without solitude.

I slipped into a booth and ordered a dry whiskey. If I planned to drink, I was going to do it right. After sliding my laptop from my duffle, I put the memory card of my camera into it and started sorting through the pictures. I had some truly wonderful images. I had worried the action shots would not be decent, but I was pleasantly surprised to see I had not lost my touch for timing.

I nixed the pictures of Grigori kissing Zoya— with Ember in the background ready to kill them. That article was not anywhere near done. I would not publish a piece on mere hearsay. I wanted real evidence that she was stepping out on Brent and Cole, and that was only the beginning of the shots I hoped to acquire.

I finally decided on two pictures, one where Grigori was setting her shoulder and the last shot of them staring down at the unconscious men. As I drained the double whiskey brought to me, ordering another, I started writing my article. It really was going to be a fluff piece, because the charity did need some recognition, but with the pictures of Ember and Grigori as the centerpiece, it would be read by all. I was just finishing my second double, and reviewing my work, when a visitor arrived at my table.

Daniil sat down directly next to me.

Sadly, I did not notice him for a few moments; I was so engrossed in my work. I sat my glass down, and was grabbing for a napkin when I bumped him. I squeaked embarrassingly.

"What the hell are you doing?" I asked, quickly hitting send on my email. My editor could finish proof reading the damn thing. I had sharks to deal with.

Daniil rested back, placing his arms over the top of the booth and stretching out his long legs. He had not changed out of his black Armani suit from the ball. I still wore my dress, since I had not dared to go back to my room.

"I'm sitting, Ms. Forter," Daniil grinned gracefully. "Your article looked lovely."

I glared. The asshole had been reading over my shoulder. "I meant, why are you sitting with me? I didn't invite you."

He lifted my glass and brought it to his nose, sniffing at the empty. His nose crinkled in disgust, and completely ignoring me, he stated, "While we chat, you and I are going to have a drink together." He placed the glass back on the table, motioning for the server. "But not the shit you were drinking."

I bristled even further, and started packing up by belongings. "I don't think so. To have a conversation that requires both people answering each other's questions. You've ignored mine so far, and insulted me." I scowled, struggling with the zipper on my duffle. "Besides, all you want to do is steal my equipment and scare me off any story I might write."

He nodded, not at all remorseful. "Yes. I do. And I will. But first, we will talk." A blatant command. I tugged harder on my zipper. The server arrived and he ordered an entire bottle of some expensive vodka I could not even pronounce—with two shot glasses.

Oh, the hell with that. I stopped struggling with my damn bag. I just needed to get out of here. But as soon as I started scooting around the booth's half-moon cushion, I felt two large hands land on my hips in an unbreakable grip, sliding me back.

I smacked at his hands. "What the hell are you doing?"

"I'm sitting, Ms. Forter. We've already established this." He parked my ass right where I had started, releasing me, and settled back against the cushion. "This will go a lot smoother if you just sit there like a good little girl and shut the fuck up."

I pointed at his face, past furious. "Look, old man. I've been intimidated and threatened by many people. It comes with the job. However, no one has ever gotten me to back off when I have a gut feeling. When I get these feelings, they always pan out. So whatever you're going to say, just save it because it's falling on deaf ears."

He swatted my finger away, his gaze just as furious as mine. "Little girl, you do realize who the fuck I am, don't you?"

I spewed, "A decrepit old man with a thug complex."

His jaw set. He stared, leaning forward, and slowly stated, "You are either very stupid or very brave to speak to me that way."

Probably both, I realized as his suit jacket opened a little, showing a gun underneath. I hated guns. Really, violence of any sort. I had actually thought twice about asking for this job when I had found out what the events were going to be.

However, I wanted to take the Donovans down. Badly.

The server sat a clear bottle of liquor down with two shot glasses.

I swallowed hard and pointed to her. I was not going to pay for that. In addition, I wanted to…his hand snaked out and landed on my thigh, keeping me in place when I tried to sneak away as he paid her. Two hundred dollars. Maybe I should steal the bottle when I finally managed my escape.

I scowled down at my lap, and started prying his pinkie finger up first from its death grip on my thigh. His ring finger. His middle. Then his pointer. I flicked his thumb last.

Hearing him chuckle, I blinked up at his gaze. The sound was low and deep, and very much masculine, and honest. I asked, "Why are you laughing?"

"Because you think you can get away." His gaze roved over me, his nose crinkling in disgust like he had done with my whiskey glass—*asshole*. He shook his head. "You'll only get hurt. Just sit, and drink with me." It was my turn to shake my head, but he held up a hand. "I'll make you a report's deal. For every two shots we each take, we'll each ask a question that has to be answered." He glanced at me while opening the vodka. "Off the record, of course."

"You want information from me?" I pushed my glasses up. "I call bullshit."

"We aren't playing Bullshit, Ms. Forter. We'll be answering each other's questions. Honestly." He poured two shots.

"I've already had two doubles. Take four to catch up." If he wanted to play this game, so be it. I was a pro at ferreting out information. I would just have to be careful how I answered his questions. This really was a reporter's dream deal. I was not too many years off my college days, and he was many from his. I was sure I could drink him under the table any day. I may be small, but I had been a freaking fish in college.

He chuckled again, making me blink a little. It

was…odd. "I really don't believe you have a clue who I am, Ms. Forter." He downed one shot. No wince. "But, I'll do as you demand." He took the other glass and downed the vodka. "This time." He refilled the glasses, and easily took the third and fourth shots.

I tried not to stare. He did not even cough. Shit.

He started to refill the glasses, but I stopped him from pouring mine. "Wait." I grabbed a napkin and started cleaning off the rim of my glass. Old man lips had touched it. I scrubbed it spotless, and sat it back on the table. "There. Filler up."

He blinked at where I held the napkin in my hand.

Did I offend him? Poor baby.

"Do you have a problem with germs?" he asked, seeming honestly confused.

Like he was God's gift to women. Idiot.

I tossed the napkin on the table. "You haven't taken two shots. I don't have to answer."

He glared and filled my shot glass. "Then let's begin."

I lifted mine for a toast.

He bypassed it, draining his.

Seriously an ass. I bristled, but still toasted against a ghost glass, and took the shot.

Well…it was chilled. And it went down. That was about all that I could say in the vodka's favor. It might as well have been fuel for a space ship.

Oh. My. Shitface.

As I coughed, and my eyes watered, he took my

glass from me and refilled it. How very kind of him. Especially, because the fucker was chuckling again. I grabbed a new napkin and dabbed at my eyes under my glasses. This was going to be hell.

Coughing from my second shot, I sat my own glass down as he gently placed his on the table, and I asked in disbelief, "And you called my whiskey shit?"

His lips twitched. "Yes. And you just wasted a question, Ms. Forter."

"No!" I pointed at him, which he quickly swatted away with irritation. "I realize English isn't your first language, but that was rhetorical."

"Not with the infliction you used. It was a question."

I ground my teeth together. *Literal old asshole.*

"Fine." Dammit, if he wasn't right. I motioned for him to ask away.

He watched me carefully. "Other than the charity event articles, what story are you literally working on?"

I glanced away. I tapped my finger on the table, thinking, and then tried not to grin, stating slowly, "The only story I'm literally working on is the charity event. That's all my editor has assigned." Take that, literal old asshole.

His teeth clenched, but he started pouring.

After two more shots for each of us, I made sure to keep my mouth shut, other than when I had to cough. I was not going to waste my question this time.

He asked immediately, "Other than the charity

event articles, what story would you hope to gain at this event?"

I sighed. I had known he would ask it again, but better stated. I only had one answer. The truth. "To catch Ember Lerrus stepping out on Brent Terrance and Cole Donovan."

Instantly. "Why?" His eyes were hard on mine.

I turned toward him and shook my head, before resting it back on the booth. "Nope. Only one question." I felt a little loose, but nowhere near tipsy. This was a good thing because he did not seem to be having any issues. "Now my question. Have Ember and Grigori ever been lovers?" The million-dollar question. "And we already established this is off the record." I just wanted the truth at this point. That would help me understand if my gut feeling was wrong.

He started twirling his glass on the table. "What do you believe constitutes as lovers?"

I rolled my eyes. "Have they had sex?"

He twirled the glass again before thumping it down and starting to pour. "I can honestly say I've never seen them have sex."

I snorted. Christ. This was going to take a shitload more shots.

Ten more shots later, I was beginning to feel it. We

were drinking them quickly, so the alcohol had not had time to fully hit, but I could tell he was even beginning to feel its effects.

He slammed his glass down, and went nose to nose with me, slurring, "Why do you care if they've had sex?"

I grinned. "I don't honestly care if they've had sex." Really, I did not. I just wanted to know if they had so I would know if I was following the right lead. I stated happily into his furious face, "My turn. Have you ever seen Ember kissing anyone besides Brent and Cole?"

Instant. "Have you seen her kissing Brent and Cole?"

I grinned. "Can't answer that. Save it for your next question. Now answer, old man."

He growled.

I laughed a little. He was kind of funny.

He sounded a bit pissed. "Yes. I've seen her kiss someone besides Brent or Cole before their miraculous return."

"Who?"

He shook his head, and started pouring.

Two shots later, I asked, "Who did you see her kiss besides Brent or Cole?"

"Her daughters."

I glared.

Once more, he put his face in front of mine. "Answer the question I asked right before."

"No. I haven't seen her kiss them." My eyebrows

came together as my fogged mind contemplated a new theory. "Why do you care if she's kissing anyone?" I gasped as the concept really manufactured in my thoughts. "Do you have a thing for Ember?"

He laughed outright, rocking on the booth.

I squinted, realizing what I was seeing.

He was really fucking handsome. Like really, really handsome.

Why had I never noticed that before?

Wait. I peered closer. Perhaps it was beer goggle vision.

Fuck...I couldn't tell.

I rubbed my forehead. "Answer my question." My words were hard to get out.

Daniil shook his head, tilting to the side. He almost fell out of the booth. I barely managed to grab his arm and yank him upright. He did not seem to notice, and went to pour, but froze. "Shit."

"You didn't answer," I demanded stubbornly, forgetting if I had already asked my one question. I glanced where he was peering. "Damn! That was good stuff, too." It really had been. In his hilarity, he must have knocked the table, because the bottle was lying on its side, the liquor spilling over the far edge of the table.

I lifted the downed bottle.

We both stared at it closely.

He muttered, "Well, shit."

I nudged his shoulder with mine. "You already said that."

"Did I?"

"I think so."

"Shit."

"Is that that all you know of the English language, old man?"

"Shit if I know."

We stared at the bottle more.

I asked, "How are we supposed to get answers now?"

His eyebrows came together. "We could order more here, but I've got something that's even better than this." His grin was crooked. "I call it Obsidian Liquor. It may be vodka, but after ingested, the resulting acts aren't pure like the liquid. It will definitely open the path to further discussion between us. Still off the record, mind you."

"No. There's no way you have something better than this." I shook the bottle. "This was fucking awesome."

"I swear." He placed a hand over his heart. "It's ten times better than that."

"Well, what are we waiting for?" I slammed the empty down. "I want answers, and you've got the Obsidian…whatever."

He chuckled and swayed as he stood. "I want the answers and I've got the liquor." His eyebrows came together again. "That should mean something."

I grabbed my bag and stumbled from the booth.

He caught my arm, mumbling, "You're a klutz."

As we made our way out of the bar, I pointed at

the tip of his nose. "You're the one that tipped the bottle."

"Shit."

"Maybe you should get a tutor." I waved grandly in greeting to his bodyguards standing at the entrance of the bar. Daniil slurred to them we needed the liquor he had brought to the resort. They wore odd expressions on their faces as they stared at us. "Are all your bodyguards ugly?" I studied them, stumbling. We both hit the wall. Their weird expressions increased as we righted ourselves. "Or maybe they need an antacid? I think I have some in my purse." I started to dig for them.

Swatting my hand away from my search, he whispered, "They're just that ugly. I hire the ugliest, scariest men I can find. Keeps the idiots at bay."

I grinned as we started walking again...but damn I forgot what I was going to say, so I asked instead, "Are you sure this stuff is better than that two hundred dollar bottle you spilled?"

We stepped into the elevator; the ugly bodyguards following inside and standing like a wall in front of us. The doors closed. Daniil answered, but I did not hear him because I was peering around the bodyguard of the right side to get a better look at them. I stumbled, but caught myself on the wall with a widespread hand, oddly, feeling things shift under it. I really did not care what I had just touched because three of the ugliest people I had ever seen before were staring at me.

I pushed away from the wall, yanking Daniil

down by his suit jacket, whispering against his ear, "The one on the left is the worst."

He pointed, and I nodded. Cocking his head, he glanced at all of them. We both forgot what I had said because the elevator dinged, and the doors opened. He and I started forward but we slammed against the wall of ugly.

Daniil barked, "Why aren't you moving?"

Least Ugly replied, "It's not our floor."

The doors closed, but no one got on. It started moving again.

"Who pressed the wrong," he waved his hand, slamming back against the wall, "thing?"

I yanked him upright. "It's called a button. Maybe I'll help find that tutor."

I could have sworn the ugly wall started shaking as the elevator door opened again.

Once more, they did not move.

Daniil asked, "Who pressed the wrong damn buttons?"

I swayed this time when the door closed and the elevator started lifting.

Daniil caught me, but we both slammed against the back wall.

We stayed there. It was safer.

The wall of ugly was vibrating again, and it looked really cool. I stared, mesmerized, and suddenly remembered that Daniil had asked a question. I thought hard, and the doors opened again, but like normal, no one moved. It hit me what he had asked, and I put my lips to his ear, not wanting them to hear, whispering, "Maybe you shouldn't have gone for ugly, but intelligence instead. Their memories aren't so good if they have to see each floor to remember where they're going."

Daniil shrugged, stating gruffly, "They can shoot and fight like demons."

I shook my head as we visited another floor. "I hate violence. Those that use it to better themselves are schmucks. Might does not make right. That point of view only creates cretin beasts."

The wall of ugly was really pulsating.

Daniil replied, "You don't really believe…" He stopped when the wall of ugly started moving out. "Ah, finally."

I pointed covertly, whispering, "The one on the left! The one on the left! He looks like an exhibit I once saw in a wax museum of horrors."

We stared, who would not, and the door started to close, but one of the guards stuck his massive paw out, making it open back up.

I whispered, "You think it's contagious?"

Daniil stared open mouthed. "You know, I never thought of it that way."

Ugly Duckling asked, "Sir? Are you getting out?"

"Yes," Daniil stated, and we both lunged through the opening at the same time, bypassing Ugly Duckling, giving him a wide berth. The man seriously had to have some kind of disease for his face to look like that.

I blinked at my surroundings. "Where are we?"

This did not look like my floor. Mine was green. This one was gold.

"Going to get the liquor," Daniil stated, pointing down one hallway.

His bodyguards took off in the opposite direction.

I cracked up when he looked miffed. "Maybe you should fire them."

He glanced left then right, calling out, "That's not the way!"

Ugly Duckling turned around, and I think his poor face looked pained.

"I really think he needs medical attention."

Daniil nodded. "I'll see to it tomorrow."

Ugly Duckling held up a room key. "Room 919. It's down this hallway."

"Think he's delusional, too?"

Daniil sighed. We walked after them, banging against walls as we went. He grumbled, "I guess we'll see."

I started singing "Friends in Low Places" by Garth Brooks.

Daniil hummed with me. His voice was not too bad.

"You like country music?"

He shrugged. "Some, but I prefer classic rock."

"Ugh. Old man stuff."

"I'm not old," he countered, harshly waving his hand in the air.

This resulted in us falling on our asses.

"Break a hip, old man?" I grumbled, getting back up to my feet.

"I'm only forty-nine," he muttered, rolling to his feet, thumping against the wall.

I tried to do the math in my head. I could not figure it out. "I'm twenty-eight. Big difference there." I paused and thought about it, Daniil stopping with me...before we started moving again. "How old were you when you had Grigori? He's what? Thirty-three?"

"Yes, he is. I was very young when he was born."

His expression went kind of sad, so I started singing "Friends in Low Places" again. That perked him up. He even sang with me this time instead of just humming. We made quite the duet until the guards stopped, and opened a door.

As I walked inside, I stared in awe, leaning against the couch. "This room rocks!"

Daniil shrugged, wobbling through the expensive living room we were in. I followed, gawking at all of the furniture, and even a tiny chandelier hanging in the middle of the room. He turned a corner next to a wall of windows that overlooked the ocean with the huge full moon shining down on it. We went down the hallway, one side a solid wall, the other the windows. There was a room at the end of the hallway with the door open.

We strolled inside. It was a bedroom with a huge bed against the opposite wall, with a nightstand on each side. A dresser was against the wall by the door, and a flat screen sitting on top of it. There was a small table set up next to the floor-to-ceiling windows with a tiny wet bar between the windows and one nightstand.

I dropped my bag and immediately maneuvered to one of the two seats at the circular glass table. The chair looked damn great after our trek through the resort. Good liquor was hard to find.

Daniil grabbed two glasses from the minibar and almost dropped them when he bent to open the fridge, but after some consideration, he bit one, holding it in his mouth while he squatted to grab one of the bottles of vodka in the fridge. When he came over, I took the glass from his mouth and set it down on the table. He poured the liquor, wobbling as he kicked the door closed.

"This had better be worth that walk," I grumbled, taking a sip. I blinked at the glass, and then glared at him. "This is fucking water!"

He tasted from his glass. His eyebrows came together until he sniffed his glass. His expression relaxed and he shook his head. "No. It's the good stuff."

I sniffed my own and could somewhat smell the alcohol. "Oh." I blinked. "Weren't we supposed to do something?"

He stared, and took a drink, draining his glass.

I followed suit.

He stated, "I don't remember."

Shrugging, I poured us more. "How about we sing? We did that well enough."

Daniil grinned, and it was sloppy crooked. "I'll teach you a song from Russia."

He proceeded to try to teach me a song from his home country. He sang it low and with gusto, and I tried to say the words, but damn, it was hard. He repeated it slowly, putting his hand on my chin, making me move my mouth differently as I said the words. I laughed when he grinned, saying I had just learned a song that would not be appropriate in respectable company.

"Weren't we using glasses?" I asked where we now stood facing the large windows and singing to the ocean, sharing the bottle between us.

He shrugged and peered at me. He swayed and his forehead bumped mine. Gradually, he tilted his head back to stare me in the eyes. "Speaking of glasses, you shouldn't wear those. They hide your eyes." He plucked them off my face, dropping them on the table and making me squint at him. "Green. Your eyes are green."

"And yours are brown. Together they make a tree." I reached for my glasses since I could not see without them. My contacts were not in my duffle.

He placed the bottle in my hand that was extending for my glasses.

I forgot what I was reaching for and took a swig.

Seriously, it tasted like water.

I asked, "What?"

He was staring at me as we swayed, bumping against one another.

"You look like a kewpie-doll without those horrid glasses," he blurted.

My nose wrinkled. "My mom collected those. I used to play with them when she wasn't around." I pointed right against the tip of his nose. "You remind me of a land shark."

He grinned. "Apt description."

I shrugged. "I thought so. But you're not so scary right now."

He chuckled, taking the bottle from me, placing it to his lips for his own swig. He tipped it back far, arching with the effort, but grunted, pulled it away from his mouth, and flipped it upside down.

We stared, blinking furiously. Shit. It was empty.

"I'll get another one," I muttered. "I drank the last of it."

I turned toward the minibar but tripped over his feet.

He caught me, but stumbled over a chair, knocking it over.

Instantly, he wrapped his arms around me, trying to catch his footing.

I squeaked, but when we landed, it was on a soft surface.

I was flat on my back on the sweet, soft bed while Daniil lay sprawled on top of me.

I muttered, "You called me a klutz?"

He lifted his head and grinned deviously. "You fell first. I saved us from the floor."

Time...wavered.

He stared down at me.

I blinked up at him.

Daniil really was gorgeous. He sure as hell did not feel like an old man against me. He felt all hard and warm. It was almost overwhelming. His shoulder length black hair hung down around his face, and his honey brown eyes were turning darker as they slowly roamed my features.

He whispered, "A minx kewpie-doll."

He lowered his face and placed his lips on mine.

My eyelids shut, and I instantly groaned as his mouth overtook mine. My lips were a little numb, so I pressed harder, yanking on his hair. He did not seem to mind, giving me want I wanted. I opened my mouth and his tongue slid in.

It was fucking good.

Instantaneously, we attacked one another's mouths and started stripping.

The next thing I remembered, I was naked on my back and he was naked on top of me.

I kissed him fiercely, and he returned the caress just as forcefully while pushing my legs apart with his knees. He reached down with one hand, his fingers landing on my core. I blinked, and the next thing I recalled, I was squirming a hand between our bodies.

Daniil jerked on top of me, taking his head off my shoulder, and stared down at me as I placed his hard cock at my core. He groaned, and pressed forward, kissing me again.

I gasped at his size as he slowly thrust into me. I

was wet, although I could not remember how I had gotten that way, but his cock was absolutely enormous. He stretched me wide, and suddenly, he licked over my lips…and thrust hard and fast, all the way in. I screamed into his mouth and he shouted, gripping fistfuls of my hair. It fucking hurt; he was so damn big.

He hissed through clenched teeth, "Fucking…itty…bitty."

My body tensed; I panted and my core stretched beyond belief.

"Give it a minute," he whispered, sounding pained.

I nodded quickly.

His lip brushed against mine, and I lost track of time all over again.

When I opened my eyes, I could still feel his cock inside me, but his head was on my shoulder while he snored softly. I started to move out from under him, but his head jerked up. While he blinked repeatedly, I slurred, "Are we done?"

He wobbled and moved his hips, and then groaned deep.

It felt so damn good as he moved that little bit, still hard.

I wrapped my legs around his waist. And he started thrusting.

It was chaotically gentle at first, and it was more than nice, but when we found our rhythm, he drove harder and rougher, and it was…amazing.

OBSIDIAN LIQUOR

With skin slapping and the headboard banging, I cried out, arching under him.

He released my hair and palmed one of my breasts, murmuring breathlessly, "All of you is bitty." He licked across my puckered nipple.

I shuddered, making his muscles quiver and he instantly nibbled at my nipple. Choking, I gripped his flexing ass as my head thrashed back and forth. He felt like pure stallion inside me.

Suddenly, I was flipped onto my belly. The room was still spinning as I was pulled up onto my knees, and from behind, he slammed his cock inside me again. He shouted my name at the same time I screamed his; his cock so fucking massive inside my core. Gripping my hips tightly, he started driving into me repeatedly. Our rhythm brutal, it felt like it went on endlessly, but still not long enough. I spread my legs wider, giving him better access.

With the head of his cock bumping my cervix and sliding farther, I shouted in pleasure.

"Christ, fucking good." He leaned over me, and bit down between my neck and shoulder, non-to-gently, and I whimpered softly, jerking when I felt two of his fingers on my clit. He moaned, licking across my skin, kissing my neck, as he pushed me further toward oblivion.

"Just a little more," I mumbled breathlessly, and he altered from circling my clit to rubbing it. I rocked, immediately screaming his name, flying over the edge.

54

My walls took hold of his cock as my muscles pulsed, my body humming with heavenly warmth.

"Fucking shit," he gasped, and started pounding into me.

My mind was floating in sizzling euphoric flames, and as his cock started to jerk inside me, hearing his husky shout of satisfaction, I passed out for good.

CHAPTER 3

Okay, so there are mornings in everyone's lives that we wish we could reason through what the fuck we had been thinking the night before.

Or, more precisely, remember the majority of the night before.

Like…

Where the fuck am I?

How did I get here?

What the hell had I done?

Most importantly, who had witnessed it?

Well…this was my morning like that.

The sun was bright against my closed eyelids, and I moaned as I lay on my rolling stomach. My head hurt like no other. Honestly, it did not even feel like my head. It just felt like a constant ball on top of my neck that pulsed with never ending pain.

I grabbed my forehead and groaned.

Then, I heard it.

Another groan. But a lot more fucking deep and masculine…right next to me.

My eyes shot open, and I blinked repeatedly through the blinding sunlight. Brown, utterly blood shot eyes, were blinking open at me. Time slowed, and flat out paused, as we stared at one another, our noses almost touching.

We both shouted.

I scooted back as fast as I could, jumping to my feet, screaming as Daniil rolled off the bed, bellowing and standing to his feet while he stared at me wide-eyed, both of us holding our heads. His gaze darted down my body just as I was doing to his.

I saw that he was fucking naked. I screamed louder and glanced down at my own body.

Shit! I was butt ass naked too.

We both dove for the down comforter. I got a good grip on it, yanking and pulling it up to my chest just as he got an end covering his, not shriveled like prunes cock and balls, the blanket like a tent over the bed as I continued to stand on it while he stood on the floor across from me.

We gawked at one another, both of us silent now.

A full minute passed in stunned quiet.

He was not providing any answers, so I started surveying the room I was in, squinting because I could not see shit without my glasses. I saw our clothing lying all around the bed, my duffle by the door, an empty bottle, and knocked over chair, plus two empty glasses on the table.

OBSIDIAN LIQUOR

Scared to do it, I moved a little on the mattress and glanced down.

An undeniable sex streak stained the black sheets. "Holy shit."

He was staring at the same spot and rubbing his forehead with his free hand. "Jesus."

I breathed deeply, and tried to remember how the fuck we had gotten here.

I gazed at him, my eyebrows coming together as he stared back.

I remembered the bar.

Something about ugly bodyguards.

Vague memories of coming into this room, his room.

Singing, maybe?

I thought harder. Yeah, there had been definite singing.

I blinked, and my jaw dropped as the memories came in a flood of the unwanted.

My gaze lowered back to his covered cock.

He had not been hard waking, but holy motherfucker I remembered when he had been.

And what we had done...

It appeared like he was beginning to remember too because his features blanked, and his gaze slowly went to my neck and down to where I held the blanket against my chest and then lower, even though he could not see anything.

I had to ask. "Did you wear a condom?"

He sucked in a large, sluggish breath, and let the

blanket fall, probably figuring, hell I had already seen it anyway. I tried to keep my gaze on his face, but my God. For an older man…shit…even for a younger man, his tan body was in incredible shape. His shoulders were wide, his muscles bulging at his biceps. His pecs were rock hard, and Jesus, he had a fucking six-pack. His waist was lean, his thighs strong as he walked, his ass rock hard, and even limp, his cock was much larger than most.

I pivoted, keeping the blanket around me as he rounded the bed, and pulled open the drawer to the nightstand that I had slept closest to. He pulled out a package of condoms. He stared, and then started spewing harshly in Russian. I spoke as calmly as I could, "I can't understand you."

He closed his eyes, holding up the package. "It's not opened." His eyes shot open and he turned to me. "Did you have any on you?"

My voice trembled when I stated simply, "No."

He rolled his shoulders. "Birth control?"

"No."

"Fuck!" he shouted, tossing the condoms back into the drawer and slamming it shut.

I, on the other hand, cringed and turned my back to him, careful to keep the blanket tight around my nude frame. I felt like crying. But fuck if I was going to do that in front of him.

He breathed harshly behind me, but he probed softly, "Tell me you've been tested."

I cleared my throat. "I get tested every six months. They've always come up clean."

"Good," he muttered. "I do the same thing with the same results."

I stilled when I heard people far outside the door. "Who's that?"

Daniil lunged across the room, standing there in all his naked glory with his ear pressed to the door. The voices were getting louder, coming closer. He glanced at the clock, and I followed his gaze. I squinted, and I could hardly read it, but I was pretty sure it said 9:33. That meant I needed to get the fuck out of here if I wanted to grab something to settle my stomach and pounding head, and still make it to the first event at 10:00.

I really, really wanted to get out of here.

Daniil grimaced, and started racing around the room shoving things under the bed. "It's my kids. They will have a shit fit if they see me naked with a woman." He grabbed my glasses and tossed them in a drawer as I stood gawking.

Was he worried about being caught with a woman in his bed?

Daniil glanced everywhere, but if he was looking for a place to hide me, he would not find it. The bathroom must be down the hall because there were no other doors in the room. Not even a closet, just a dresser. "Shit." He glanced at the door as they got even closer, arguing with his bodyguards by the sound of it.

It was not just his kids, because I heard what sounded like Stash and Zane speaking too. "Lay down flat."

I just stood staring at him in shock.

He growled, springing at me and covering my mouth as I squeaked.

I gaped wide-eyed, frozen, as he positioned me flat on my back and centered on the bed…right before he yanked the comforter away from me, diving down on top of me. I panted breathlessly as he lay naked on top of me. "We are not having sex again!"

He snorted. "No shit." I glared as he arranged pillows around my head, covering all but my face, and he muttered, "Thank God you're bitty."

He froze.

I stilled.

I remembered him saying that to me about a certain part of my anatomy.

He cleared his throat, his eyes darting to mine for a second before his expression hardened again, his nose crinkling, and he turned his attention to spreading the comforter out right. "Now be still." He rested his head to the side—directly above my nose—putting his arms on either side of my face on top of the pillows.

I tried to breathe normally, but Christ, he was heavy and squashing me horribly. I had no time to complain unless I wanted everyone to know that I had slept with Grigori's dad, because by the sound of it, even as the bodyguards argued with them, Artur, Eva, Stash, and Zane barged into the room.

Daniil had closed his eyes and was softly pretending to snore. It was pretty realistic.

I breathed shallowly, trying not to blow his hair too badly.

Eva coughed hard, muttering, "Jesus. It smells like a distillery in here."

Daniil blinked his eyes open, barely moving his head to the side. "What the fuck is everyone doing in here?"

A flurry of movement. It sounded like some left, probably the guards.

"It's about Zoya. We think Ember poisoned her last night," Artur stated instantly, oddly, sounding pleased with that bit of news.

I stilled completely.

Oh. If he was happy with the news, he was not the only one. That was fucking perfect.

Daniil froze when I did, and he started speaking quickly in Russian.

I pinched his thigh hard where my hand rested. The asshole was not going to start that shit up again. He words faltered as he grunted, moving his legs between mine, and started talking again…still in Russian.

His cock rested against my core, and unbelievably, as everyone in the fucking room spoke to one another in a language I did not understand, he started to get hard. I lifted my head a smidge and bit his earlobe. I wanted him the fuck off me…even if, by some delirious miracle, the sex had been great from what I could remember.

He grunted, and quickly cleared his throat, even as I bit harder, and he stated rapidly in English, "I'll meet you downstairs in fifteen minutes."

It did not sound like they wanted to leave, but Stash got them moving.

They said their farewells; except for…Daniil did not move.

I bit him harder, but he only pressed down more firmly on me.

I quickly realized why.

The door shut, and Zane, who apparently had stayed in the room, said quietly, "Daniil, whoever's under you right now had better keep her fucking mouth shut about what she just heard." His tone was a complete honest threat. "If she doesn't…I. Will. Ruin. Her."

Daniil turned his head, just enough to stare me in the eyes, but not enough for Zane to see me. "You have nothing to worry about, Zane, because I will ruin her myself before you would ever need to if she says anything to anyone." Shark. He was most categorically a killer shark staring down at me with that deadly gaze, even if he was hard down below.

"Good. And your kids didn't notice. Stash kicked her bra completely under the bed before they saw it," Zane commented.

Daniil nodded, still with his eyes on mine.

Zane left, gently shutting the door behind him.

I was angry, and more than a little scared, staring back at Daniil, and I only waited a heartbeat before hissing, "Get the fuck off me."

His teeth bared. Definitely a damn shark. "Will you keep your mouth shut, Ms. Forter?"

Slowly, knowing I shouldn't, but not able to stop myself, I opened my mouth wide.

I left it that way. *Fuck you, old man.*

His nostrils flared. He glared, his cheeks flushing, right before he shouted, "Are you as crazy as your fucking hair? I could break your neck, shoot you, suffocate you, beat you, or slit your throat, all without a second thought. And yet, you still try to piss me off?"

I squirmed, my heart in my throat. He had officially scared the shit out of me. He stared with a look I had not seen in his eyes before. His gaze told me he was telling the truth. He would murder me without an ounce of remorse. I could not breathe with him on me, and I pushed as hard as I could against his chest, digging my heels into the mattress, shoving back. All that got me was…nowhere…and a laugh from him.

Still chuckling, he gripped my face. I tried to jerk away, starting to hyperventilate, but he just gripped tighter, his fingers digging into my scalp. "Do you really think you can get away from me that easily?" He shook his head. "I told you last night you would only get hurt doing that, and now look at you. You can barely breathe; you're so scared." He chuckled as if it was the funniest thing he had heard.

I gasped, "You're crazy." I had slept with a crazy man. An old crazy man.

What the hell had I been thinking?

A full-fledged freak out was on its way. I could feel it, staring up at the man with death eyes and a laughing mouth. It began to edge out, a complete breakdown like I had not had since my father had caught me having sex that first time. I had to get away from this man.

He clamped a hand over my mouth, just as I was getting ready to scream. His smile was instantly gone, only a stone cold killer staring back at me as he murmured quietly, "Now do you understand who I am, Ms. Forter? Will you keep your mouth shut?"

My breath was coming hard and fast, and I felt like I was going to faint, but I was smart enough to nod. Yes, I would keep my mouth shut. Especially, as he lay on top of me with a hard cock and my death in his eyes.

"Good." He took his hand off my mouth, rolling off the bed and me. "Maybe you're smarter than you appear."

I quickly brushed the tears away that had escaped, and holding the blanket against me, moved until I fell off the bed. On the side he was not on. It hurt my knees, but I kept low, reaching a trembling hand under the bed, grabbing anything I felt and yanking it out until I found all of my clothes and duffle. I was trembling so badly it was difficult to get my clothes on under the cover, and my stupid tears would not stop flowing, but

I did it as fast as possible. I needed to get away from the violence he promised.

When I had my bra, panties, and dress on, I grabbed my heels, slinging my duffle over my shoulder and brushed the blanket aside. I did not glance anywhere near him as he stood silent, watching me, as I raced across the room, banging into the dresser where he had hid my glasses. Yanking the drawer almost all the way out, I grabbed them, managing not to crush them as I put them on. They instantly fogged from my tears and heated skin, and I had to yank them back off. Fuck it. I did not need to see perfectly to leave.

Not looking back, I ran out of the room and down the hallway. The bodyguards were sitting on the couch, watching TV. All three of them observed me as I raced across the living room, fumbling with the door handle and fighting a losing battle with wiping my tears away. I hated it when my dad's advice was right. Go looking for trouble, which I did on a normal basis with my job, and it will find you even sooner.

I threw the door open and raced out of the room...only to run into a wall.

A Zane wall.

Starting to fall, he grabbed my arms, easily keeping me on my feet.

I jerked out of his hold when I was steady, wiping tears away again with the back of my shaking hand that held my shoes and glasses. I glanced away from his completely shocked face.

Yeah. It was me.

He recovered well enough, clearing his throat. "I was going to tell the women that exited his room that I was honest in my threat." He paused, staring. I would not look at him, but I could feel his penetrating gaze on my face. "I'm still honest in it, but I don't think you need to hear that."

My chin wobbled as I remembered what Daniil had said.

The ways he would kill me.

After having sex with me the night before.

My eyes burned as fresh tears fell, and my throat clogged so hard I had to clear it. I nodded once before dodging past him and running full out down the hallway without a clue if it was even the right direction, my black dress pressing against my front and blowing out behind me. I just needed to get the fuck away.

"No way, Elizabeth. Everyone's busy. They have their assignments. You begged for this. Now you have it. Suck it up," my editor, Clifford, barked into my ear. Then he hung up on me.

I gazed at my phone, jumping as someone bumped my arm outside the arena entrance.

I could not calm down, and it appeared, I could not get out of this fucking assignment.

I cursed, throwing my phone into my purse. I dug

through it until I found the aspirin at the bottom and a water bottle with just enough moisture left in it to down as much medicine as I dared. My head hurt; my eyes were dry and scratchy-to go right along with my throat-since I had bawled while I was in the shower.

Now, I had to go back in with the man that had made it all possible.

Throwing my empty water bottle into a trashcan, I pushed my sunglasses up on my nose; I had put my contacts in, making my eyes hurt worse. I could not let anyone see how horribly blood shot my eyes were even after the puffiness had gone down from my crying jag. The vodka had certainly not done my body good. I pulled at my half-turtleneck, sleeveless ribbed blouse, making sure the fucking hickie Daniil had given me on the bottom of my neck was covered. The damn thing was huge with tiny little bruises of teeth marks around it where he had bitten me before sucking.

I sighed and rolled my neck, opening one of the doors to the event that was already taking place inside. I was an hour late. Other than the sunglasses, I, at least, appeared like a professional, my wild curls excluded since they were an aberration to human kind. I knew there was music blaring inside, but after stepping into the room designed for this morning group sparring defense event, I immediately wanted to leave.

Loud rock music was not conducive to a hangover.

I rubbed my temples and walked forward through the bleachers. I already had a program and knew Lion

Security would be paired against Ploya Vie Security's finest in a half hours' time. There were two groups going at it right now, one attacking the other that stood in the middle. I did not peer too closely. I was not feeling warm and cozy with violence right now.

Glancing about the room, I saw where the members of the press were seated. I quickly made my way there, crossing in front of a bleacher where celebrities cheered, making my head hurt even worse. I felt like I was going to throw up. But I never did that. Puking was just not healthy in my opinion.

I could not see any great seat, so I merely headed toward the closest one I saw. I waded through the folded chairs, the fellow press members yelling at me as I got in the way of their shots. Ignoring them because I did not want to talk to anyone, I sat down on a hard seat, and without excitement took out my camera. I lifted it to my face, but my sunglasses got in the way of seeing anything decent.

Cracking my neck, I pushed my sunglasses on top of my head, since it was dark around the edges of the room where I sat. There was only a spotlight in the center of the large room, showing the fighters to full effect. I was able to snap a few shots before the fight ended.

Mrs. Donovan and the Mayor spoke as medical personnel, and members of the competitors groups that had not participated in this round, helped those injured off the floor.

I turned on my seat, not looking anywhere near

the family section, glancing up at the bleachers where the competing groups were sitting like before. I found the hot pink shirts, and put the camera to my face and started taking photos of Brent, Cole, Ember, and Grigori, the ones that would sell the most newspapers right now. Ember appeared to be arguing with Zane, who was shaking his head at her, his expression stern, and the other three were just watching Mrs. Donovan and the Mayor speak.

I figured out why Ember was irritated. Apparently, she was not going to fight in this particular event. She appeared furious as she stood on the sidelines with a few others from Lion Security. Everyone else from L.S. was out in the middle of the floor, situating themselves in a circle with their backs to one another.

The fight was on, with more pain-inducing music blaring over the speakers.

The Ploya Vie Security's group of competitors charged them.

I really wanted to ask if it was a joke at the end. It had been three to one against Lion Security, but not even ten minutes later every single one of the people that had attacked them were on the ground, while every single one of the L.S. members still stood on their feet. They might look a little rough around the edges, but they had kicked their opponent's ass without any of their blood being shed.

I stood on my chair, getting a higher angle, and snapped as many photos as I could of their circle with the fallen all around them. I definitely had my next photo for the fluff piece I would need to send tonight. I was not sure if I was still going to pursue Grigori or Ember's possible love affair. I knew I was not going to mention a damn thing about a possible poisoning, for the main reason that I liked to breathe…and the story was only hearsay, not actually fact.

For now, I would play the good little reporter and do what my editor had demanded.

As I was leaving the arena, I was completely surprised when Ember approached me. I pushed my sunglasses up on my nose and stopped, waiting to hear what she had to say. I was in no mood to deal with anyone right now. Not even whom I had come here to follow.

Ember opened her mouth and slowly shut it. She stared. "Um…"

I waited.

Her eyebrows lowered, and her eyes went freaky as she assessed me. "Never mind."

She turned to leave.

I sighed, grabbing her arm. I must really look like shit. "What do you want, Ms. Lerrus?"

She stared again with that freaky-deaky scrutiny.

I motioned for her to hurry up. She was a weird one.

Her eyes swung to the people passing by on either side of us where they exited through the arena doors—the doors that I had not made it through quickly enough. She grabbed my hand and tugged me out of the mainstream traffic. When we were on the sidelines, she leaned in, whispering, "I know this is an odd request, but is there any way I can get a copy of that photo you took of Grigori and Zoya kissing at the ball?" She batted her eyelashes. "I want to give it to them as a present."

I kept my features blank. It was not hard with my current mood, even though I knew she was lying out her ass. I shrugged. "Sure. After it's published." I was not going to give it to her before then. How stupid did she think I was? It was a prime shot. Moreover, if she saw what she looked like in it beforehand, she would try to stop me from publishing it.

I turned to leave, but this time she grabbed my arm, stopping me. I sighed and turned back to her. And froze. My eyes went huge. I gulped, my heart rate instantly galloping. I started to tremble, and Ember stilled; her hand dropped from my arm as she glanced over her shoulder where I was staring. Daniil had already glanced away from us, speaking with Zane and Lev, but he stood not even fifteen feet behind her. He had been staring before, right at me with that deadly look in his eyes.

I sucked in a breath and altered my attention back to Ember, who was still staring over her shoulder. I stated quickly, "I've got to go."

Again, her hand snaked out without looking and she gripped my forearm with bruising force, not letting me leave. I yanked, but she held on, slowly turning her gaze back to me. She said the magic words that made me stay in place. "If you go to lunch with me, so I can try to convince you to give me a copy of that photo now, I'll give you an exclusive interview with me. Any fifteen questions that you want to ask. On the record."

I stilled, my trembling completely stopped. She never talked to the press, not when Jonah Boydson, her late husband, had died, or when her father had died in the same freak murders. Or even when Brent and Cole, her previous and current boyfriends had come back from the dead. No one had been able to get her to sit down for an interview. This was like the Holy Grail of opportunities. And she was offering it to me. I knew the woman had to hate me from my past articles. It was more than disbelieving.

"Why don't you just try to steal it?" I had no doubt she was capable of that.

She shrugged, considering me. "I'm not a bitch all the time, just like you're not." She stared me in the eyes; the eerie look gone. "You took the photo. That's your job. I figure we can work something out instead of having to resort to other means. Plus, I need to give an interview soon. The press won't quit hounding me, so it might as well be you." She smirked, sort of. "It might keep you from spying outside our gates."

I chuckled, because that was probably true. "Fine. I'll go to lunch with you and listen to your spiel, but I'm not promising the photo." I stuck my hand out. "In return, you'll give me a fifteen question interview, on the record, in two weeks' time." I specified a time frame.

She snorted, and shook my hand. "Deal. Sucks you put that last bit on there."

I shrugged, taking my hand back. "I don't like getting screwed by details."

Lev approached, placing his arm over Ember's shoulders.

Ember leaned quickly so she could whisper against my ear, "But you can't tell a soul that I want that photo; if you do, the deals off. Just say you're going to interview me after lunch."

I nodded. If that was her demand, then so be it. I'd had worse stipulations before.

She stepped back under Lev's arm, and rested against him. That was when I noticed others were strolling our way. I did not look at any of the faces moving toward us, just stared at their shoulders. I saw Daniil's among the bunch of too broad frames. He was wearing a turtleneck, like mine, but black instead of cream and his shirt had sleeves.

Glancing at Ember, I jerked my head toward the doors. "We better go. You guys only have two hours for lunch."

Ember lifted away from Lev's side when Brent and Cole came up behind her. "We'll be eating with my group. You'll be joining us at a little place in town."

I peered at the ground as Daniil, Stash, Zane,

Grigori, and hell, everyone else in her group stopped behind them. I sucked in a breath, and tried not to puke. I did not glance up, mumbling, "How about we eat somewhere else. Alone. It'll give us a better chance to talk if everyone isn't around." She had said she wanted to persuade me to hand over the photo.

"Ember?" Zane asked calmly. "Is Ms. Forter bothering you?"

I peeked up to glare at him. I was not bothering her. She was bothering me.

"No," Ember stated slowly. "Ms. Forter will be joining us for lunch today. I'm going to be giving my first interview to her after we eat. It'll save on time that way." I had angled my body so I did not have to look at Daniil, and still give myself an escape route. Ember shrugged her shoulders, speaking to me, "I would rather have lunch with everyone else. You have to understand that I would prefer their company over…" She said just enough to let me know that she honestly did not like me. She may not be a bitch all the time, but she could be one. And she was letting it show.

The situation all around was more than distressing. I did not want to be anywhere near Daniil, and I hated when people were flat out rude to me when they had other people backing them, like the in-crowd versus the geeks. My stomach was rolling. I swallowed hard, and adjusted my stance when I saw Daniil's shoulders move.

I breathed deeply, and tried to keep my face blank as all of these fit, beautiful people stared. My father's advice suddenly flittered through my thoughts again. I was not exactly looking for trouble, but if I went with them, I would be. Holy Grail or not, I wanted to stay breathing. I shook my head and took a step back. "I'm sorry, Ms. Lerrus. I just remembered I have a previous engagement. Thank you for the opportunity, though."

I took another step back, and turned to go, ignoring how most of them wore shocked expressions. I was a little stunned myself. I hated that I was turning tail and running.

"Ms. Forter...," Ember stated loudly. "Twenty-five instead of fifteen."

I froze in place. *Shit.* Twenty-five fucking questions I could ask her.

Brent asked softly, "What are you doing, darlin'?"

"I want her to do the damn article. No one will bother me after she does it."

I cracked my neck.

Well...hell.

Father was not always right.

I turned, focusing solely on her. "My other engagement can wait. Let's eat."

CHAPTER 4

I thanked God my new rental car had been delivered this morning. So on the way to the restaurant, I did not have to ride with them. I just followed all of their expensive rentals into town. Unfortunately, as luck would have it, my new rental's air conditioning was not working.

I was a sweating mess when I entered the restaurant at the back of their group. I had it in mind to sit as far away from Ember as I could, so that she could not convince me to give up the photo. She was bizarre enough to be able to do so. When everyone began sitting at the huge table in the open and airy restaurant that was painted white-as in everything in the place was white, except for a few splashes of blue here or there-I purposely dropped my purse, giving someone else a chance to take my seat next to her.

Lev hopped onto it quickly. I mentally made a note of that.

When I straightened, slinging my purse over the

same arm as my duffle, I stared at the back of Lev's head in fake surprise, then glanced around the table, playing the part perfectly...until...*shit*. Until the only fucking seat left was right between Daniil and Zane.

I swallowed, and quickly tapped Lev's shoulder. "Can I sit next to Ember, please?"

Ember glanced to him, her hooded gaze pleading, just for his eyes. But I saw it.

He shook his head, not even glancing at her. "I don't think so. She said the interview wasn't until after lunch. Not during. I'm not going to let you hound her while she eats."

"It's all right, Lev," Ember stated quietly. "Let her sit there."

He shook his head, still scowling at me. "Find another seat."

"Lev..." Ember mumbled.

"Honey, I agree. You need to eat without being bothered. Build up your strength for the next event," Cole murmured quietly, resting his arm on the back of her chair.

Her eyes closed for a second. She paused, and then nodded.

Dammit.

I kept my gaze on my 'new' assigned chair and gradually made my way to it. This was possibly the worst situation that could have occurred. That was what I got for trying to renege on a deal. Being sneaky was not my strong suit. I was still learning.

Zane pulled my chair out for me.

I did not say thank you. The asshole had just threatened me a few hours ago. I pushed my sunglasses up on my nose. It was not quite bright enough in here for them, but I still wore them after a quick glance earlier in the rearview mirror had shown my eyes were still horribly bloodshot. I started tugging my purse and duffle off my shoulder.

I paused when Kirill, a Russian friend of the Kozar's, who was seated across the table from me, whistled loudly. I looked up, and he was staring. Everyone's attention went instantly from him to me; they all seemed freakily in sync with one another and they all stared.

At me. Or, more precisely, my neck.

I quickly pulled my duffle and purse the rest of the way off, stuffing them under the table, and readjusted my turtleneck that had been tugged down just enough to show my hickie.

Kirill stated, "It looks like someone took a long bite out of you." His accent was very heavy, and I really had to pay attention to understand.

But I did. It was embarrassing as hell because it was very fucking true.

"Christ," Chloe, an employee of Lion Security *and* Kirill's girlfriend, stated loudly next to him as I slowly took my seat, keeping my hands on my lap, away from Zane and Daniil. "I only thought Russians made those so dark." Her eyes darted to mine as I kept utterly still, trying my hardest not to gawk at her. "Your man's not from Russia is he?"

I blinked. My God, this was fucking awful.

She laughed, glancing around the table as some of them snickered. "Artur, Roman, is there something you need to tell us?"

Even worse. She went straight to Daniil's fucking kids that were right around my age.

"Chloe…" Zane stated quietly, but harshly, as Roman and Artur laughed, shaking their heads. "That's enough."

She appeared stunned at the order before her face shut down with nothing showing.

Kirill did not like that much. He stood up sharply. "What the hell's your problem?"

I held up my hands. "Please, stop." My hands were shaking, and I quickly put them back on my lap. "There's no need to argue over this." I shuddered. I could not take any violence right now. I already felt more than a little faint. Kirill sat slowly when Zane did not meet his challenge, and I looked at Chloe. "Honestly, I didn't really know the guy. We were drunk, and when the alcohol wore off neither one of us were pleased with the outcome. So if you don't mind, I would appreciate it if," I glanced around the table, "everyone would drop it."

Lev nodded politely, gesturing to my face. "That explains the sunglasses."

"Yeah. That explains the sunglasses." I breathed deeply, and grabbed for my purse under the table, leaning Zane's way, the lesser of two evils since he had just stuck up for me.

OBSIDIAN LIQUOR

I needed more aspirin for this.

A turkey sandwich and coleslaw were placed in front of me. It did not look appealing at all, even though I had ordered it specifically since it was not seafood, which almost the entire menu was. I turned the plate in a circle, being careful not to bump anyone's elbows, and noticed that Daniil had gotten ribs and fries. That had been my second choice, but I had selected this entree instead. Now, I wished I had not because his smelled delicious.

I peeked under the bread of my sandwich, and miserably saw that it had mustard on it. The menu had not stated that or I would have definitely ordered it without. I was one hell of a picky eater, and if food was set in front of me that was not what I really liked, I would not eat it. I would rather starve. Someone once told me I really did not know what it was like to go hungry then, which was probably true, but I still was not going to eat it. I sighed, letting the bread fall back onto the turkey, and lifted the Bloody Mary I had ordered. This was the best hangover medicine around, my tried and true remedy.

Sipping it, I almost spit it out. *Christ!* There was no vodka mixed in.

I twisted on my seat, waving the waitress down.

When she arrived, I handed her the glass. "I think you forgot the liquor. There's no vodka in there." That smidge of vodka was going to help. Without it, it tasted like tomato soup. And bad tomato soup, at that.

She paused. "I'm sorry, ma'am. Our shipment of vodka didn't make it this morning."

I stared. The woman had given me a virgin. No tip for her. "I guess whisky will work."

She shook her head. "We're out of that, too."

This place was going to lose a lot of cash from their delayed shipment. "Okay…how about a beer? Any kind is fine." I had done that few times. It was not so bad.

Again, she shook her head. "Sorry. We're out of that, too."

I blinked, and then scanned our table, gradually peering back to her. Half the occupants at the table were having beer with their lunch. They were staring at her as I was. I had figured out before our food was served they were a very nosy group, listening to other conversations.

"You're out of beer?" I asked flatly. I gestured toward the table. "What's all that?"

"The last of it," she stated quickly, handing me back my virgin Bloody Mary. "I'm very sorry for the inconvenience." She pivoted and walked away.

What the fuck?

I stared after her as the conversation started up again at my table, and I could have sworn I saw someone walk away from the bar with what looked like an alcoholic beverage.

With my eyebrows together, I turned and set my disgusting drink down. And froze, staring at my plate. It was ribs and fries. I glanced to my right, and saw Daniil's hand with a fork in it, scooping up slaw from the plate directly in front of him.

I covertly eyed his hand as it moved up, and watched as he ate the slaw-with a tiny grimace. He put his fork down, and lifted the sandwich, taking a bite. Again, he chewed with another frown, but he continued eating it. I looked back down at my plate. My *new* plate.

When the hell had he done that? More importantly, why?

I heard a quiet chuckle from my left, and I glanced at Zane.

He cleared his throat, taking a sip of his beer. His dark eyes were utterly amused as I stared at him wide-eyed, even though he could not see it behind my glasses. He tilted his beer toward me. "You wanna put some of my beer in your drink?"

Thump.

My head snapped down at the sound, and I saw my virgin Bloody Mary sitting on its side, the red mixture spilled all over the white tablecloth. "No. I guess not, but thank you." I quickly righted the cup, and grabbed my napkin from my lap, trying to clean the mess the best I could. I had not even realized that I had bumped my *new* plate against the glass. Maybe Daniil was right. I was being a little klutzy. I was confused as hell about my *new* plate of food, but the scent was all types of appealing and Daniil was eating everything off my *old* one. So I dug in.

It was fabulous.

I moaned a little as I ate, my stomach finally settling.

"Ms. Forter…" Ember's eyebrows came together. "You know, can I just call you Elizabeth?" I nodded, and she continued. "Thank you. So, Elizabeth, you seemed a little uneasy when Kirill tried to," her hands fluttered, "intimidate Zane earlier. Is there a reason you don't like fighting?" She gestured at the other members of L.S. "Because we all do, as you've been watching at the events."

I cleared my throat and searched for a napkin. There was one between Daniil's plate and mine, so I grabbed it, wiping my mouth off, and then my fingers. "Growing up, my parents disapproved of violence. I've followed in their footsteps on that point of view." Christ, the BBQ sauce was hard to get off.

She cocked her head, murmuring like she was talking to herself, "Your parents." She blinked, nodding for some reason. "What exactly do your parents do for a living?"

My stomach full, I rested back on my chair. "My mother's a director for one of the largest anti-gun coalition companies in the United States." I sat the now stained napkin down on the table. "And my father's a preacher."

Zane started choking on my left.

Daniil began having a coughing fit on my right.

The rest of them stared at me in silence.

Zoya, who looked decidedly ill today, snapped out of it first, offering Daniil a glass of water since he was still coughing. I took my cue from her, and passed Zane his beer since he was making an odd sound in his throat. I glanced back at everyone; well, everyone except for Daniil, who was somewhat quieting down.

What did I say wrong?

Grigori cleared his throat, relaxing on his seat and placing his arm on the back of Zoya's chair. "Do you still attend church? And believe in your mother's views?"

I nodded slowly. "Yes." It felt like I was digging myself into an early grave.

Stash blinked. "So guns make you feel uncomfortable?"

"More than uncomfortable."

"You go to church, like, every Sunday?" Roman asked, appearing bewildered.

"Yes, when I'm not out on assignment."

Complete extended quiet.

Chloe cleared her throat, placing her hands on the table. "Okay, let me ask you a hypothetical question. You're put in a room where a single gun sits on a table directly between you and a man who you know is going to kill you if he reaches it first. What would you do?"

I blinked, my eyebrows coming together. "I have no clue."

Everyone stared.

Anna jolted on her seat, and stated like she was being helpful, "But she doesn't have all of her parents' views." Heads snapped to her, and her cheeks flushed, but she tapped her neck, and then gestured toward me. Heads jerked back to me, and stared at my covered hickie.

I chuckled. "No. I'm not a nun. I already said it was their views about violence I agree with, not my parents' every viewpoint."

They still stared.

My stomach churned once again, feeling incredibly uncomfortable as they gaped. I did not know what the hell their problem was. They were gawking at me as if I had leprosy. I cleared my throat, and glanced to Ember. "I think I'll take that interview later tonight. I'm going to head back to the resort." I scooted my chair and lifted my duffle and purse from under the table.

Standing, while they still stared, I placed cash on the table, and turned to leave. Beginning to walk down the line of gawkers, I was suddenly shoved in the chest hard as shit. My body went airborne, flying backward. I hit the floor back first, my breath gone as a man instantly landed on top of me. I threw my hands up... but I was not fast enough. A fist slammed against the side of my face. At least, I think it was a fist. It came out of nowhere, and I could not see anything for a moment, like time literally paused. I was pretty sure I blacked out for a second.

Just as rapidly, there was no one on top of me and I was being lifted off the ground.

I gasped for air, blinking the haze from my eyes, clinging to whatever man's shirt that was holding me. All I knew was that the person that had lifted me was not attacking me. I wheezed and coughed hard. My chest burned even as little sparkles floated in my vision against the hot pink shirt I was resting against. A hand started rubbing my back, and I shook my head, sounds beginning to register.

There were people shouting, and I tilted my head up when I was finally able to get a decent breath. Lev held me, talking soothingly even while his eyes kept darting over my head. Sucking air, I turned in his embrace, not certain if I could stand completely on my own yet. I held my cheek, feeling blood and wincing as the side of my face throbbed like hell.

Immediately, I pushed farther back against Lev when I saw what was happening.

On the white tiled floor, not even five feet away, was the man who had attacked me.

He had company down there with him.

Daniil had a hand around my assailant's throat so he could not breathe. Stash pressed his own forearm against my attacker's chest so he could not move. Grigori was slamming the man's hands on the ground above his head, in order to make him release the knife he held. Carl held his legs so he could not kick. Everyone else who had been at my table was standing with a gun aimed at him.

I began hyperventilating, sucking in air too fast and too hard.

Where the fuck had all those guns come from?

Daniil spoke harshly in Russian to his and Grigori's bodyguards, who had started to hover. They nodded and began herding people out of the restaurant. Even the workers were ordered to leave. They did so quickly, gaping at all the weapons. I was ready to run with them. I was full out trembling and wheezing by the time the last person left the establishment. When the door shut, Daniil reached behind his back...and pulled out his own fucking gun.

He placed it against the man's forehead.

The rest of the group put theirs away, watching calmly.

I closed my eyes and tried to breathe evenly. I could not speak if I could not breathe.

Daniil asked coolly, "Who are you?"

"Brad Fink," the man rasped.

"Who sent you?" Daniil probed, which I thought was an odd question.

Silence.

I finally got enough air into my lungs, and made myself not stare at the gun pointed at my accoster's head as I opened my eyes. I focused on Daniil's face. "Stop. Don't kill him."

He paused. "Do you know him?"

"No."

He kept his attention on the man. "I'll only ask

you one more time, Mr. Fink." His gaze was lethal. "Who sent you?"

The man whimpered, jerking, his hands shaking under Grigori's death grip.

My eyes filled with tears. Daniil was seriously going to kill the guy. It was there in his unsympathetic scrutiny. I stared directly into my assailant's eyes. "Do you know the name of the person who sent you?"

His head shook slightly, his eyes darting everywhere. "No. He just paid me a thousand dollars to snatch your bag."

I stared until I shoved out of Lev's hold, dipping to pick my duffle off the floor.

Daniil asked, "Where and when are you supposed to meet this man?"

"Chest Lane and 43rd St. Red Buick. Fifteen minutes," he panted.

Daniil put his gun away. "Thank you for being truthful." He slammed his fist down against the man's face.

I jerked back, and Lev kept me from falling. Blood spewed from the unconscious man's broken nose. I swallowed down the bile that rose against the back of my throat. He lay as if he were dead even as Grigori, Stash, Carl, and Daniil released him.

I stared back and forth from the prone man to Daniil, wide-eyed, belatedly realizing my sunglasses were long gone. Probably when I had been punched. Blinking rapidly, I watched as Daniil grabbed a napkin to clean the blood off his hand while everyone began talking at once.

Glancing at Lev, I asked, "Isn't anyone going to call an ambulance for that guy?" Hell, if I knew where my damn purse had dropped, I would do it.

Lev stared down at me calmly. "No."

I jerked out of his hold, and pushed through the men that had held my attacker down and dropped to my knees, feeling for his pulse with my free hand, my other still pressed against my cheek. I found it, breathing a sigh of relief, and then I was jerked off my knees to stand shakily on my feet. Daniil released my arms when I was steady.

He grabbed my hand, pulling it from my face.

I stood a little shocked for two reasons.

One, Daniil tilted my chin, inspecting my cheek with terrifying eyes, but he was gentle.

Two, there was a lot of fucking blood on my hand that he had pulled away.

I was not positive what stunned me more.

He cursed softly, turning his head and speaking in Russian to one of his bodyguards, who nodded and walked away. His brown eyes met mine and trapped me. "You may not like fighting or guns, Ms. Forter, but it just saved your life. That man was an inch away from slitting your throat; and all for a thousand dollars." He dropped his hands from my face and squatted, grabbing one of the man's arms and yanking his sleeve up. He pointed, and I stared at the recent track marks from an obvious drug addiction. "He would have killed you in plain view of everyone just to score his next fix." He tossed the man's arm aside, standing. "You should think about that the next time you question if violence is a necessary evil." Glaring, he turned his back to me, and joined the discussion about what should be done.

I stood in shock, staring down at the man who had almost killed me. I started shaking as I watched the blood begin to change from a steady flow to a trickle from his busted nose. This was not the first time I had been attacked in my line of work. I had once spent two weeks in a hospital from so many broken bones after I was mugged and beaten for a CD I'd had on me that contained information about a financial company cheating the I.R.S. That did not make this time any better. I was still freaked the hell out.

Someone brushed my arm, and I yelped loudly, jumping away from the touch. Standing with my feet shoulder width apart, I rested on the balls of my feet ready to sprint away. The room went silent. As my breath rushed from my lungs, I realized the bodyguard Daniil had spoken with was who had touched me. He was holding a bag of ice in his large paw. I stared wide-eyed at the ice as he lifted it higher.

He spoke with a heavier accent than Kirill. "This is for you, Ms. Forter. For your cheek."

I blinked, and then giggled, feeling more than a little overwhelmed. I slapped a hand over my mouth to stop it. I breathed deeply, and from behind my hand, I murmured, "Please don't sneak up on me like that again."

"I'm sorry, miss. I didn't mean to frighten you," he stated softly, extending his hand.

I realized he was Ugly Duckling.

He was not any better looking while I was sober. But he seemed sweet.

I lowered my hand and took the ice, smiling kindly, even though the movement made my cheek hurt like hell. "No harm, no foul."

His lips curled the tiniest bit, and it was even more dreadful and frightening, but I widened my smile because I did not think the man smiled very often. I did not want to scare him away from it. Everyone needed to smile once in a while. It was good for the soul.

I lifted the bag of ice to my cheek and flinched, but I kept it there. Slowly, I realized the room was still quiet. I glanced over my shoulder.

Everyone was staring mutely and wearing the oddest expressions.

Chloe's mouth was gaping, and she pointed at the guard behind me. "Is he the guy you slept with last night? It would make sense for the Russian hickie you've got." She stared over my head. "I've never seen him smile before."

My eyes practically bulged wide, even as everyone's jaws went slack while they stared over my head at Ugly Duckling. Well, except for Zane and Daniil. They were staring at him, but with hooded gazes. I could not read their expressions.

A deep chuckle sounded behind me. "She and I

OBSIDIAN LIQUOR

have not slept together. Although, I would not be opposed to it if she wished it so."

I had the good sense to hood my own gaze, and shut my mouth before anyone glanced in my direction. This situation was just a smidge too crazy for me. They were glancing back and forth between the two of us; Zane was choking again, and Daniil was staring at his bodyguard with a hand over his mouth while he rested his elbow on an arm crossed over his chest.

I pointed at the man prone on the ground. "I think we have more important things to worry about than who I slept with last night and who my next partner is going to be. Is he still alive?" Everyone blinked a few times, and I kept my gaze firmly away from Daniil, who was still silent, and Zane, who was slowly gaining control over himself.

Artur looked down at the man. He kicked him in the ribs. Hard. The guy groaned in his unconscious state. Artur glanced at me. "He's alive."

I stared, holding the bag of ice to my cheek. He was as crazy as his dad was. I cleared my throat. "How about in the future I check his vitals?"

Ember was watching me closely. She motioned to the guy on the ground. "Elizabeth, would you like us to take care of this quietly? We're looking for a little fun in Key West, so we'll do it pro-bono between events. Find out who set this up."

I knew what she really wanted. Pro-bono, my ass. I smiled sweetly. "Thank you, but I don't think so. The police will be here any minute with you people pulling your guns like you did. I'll let the authorities handle it."

Her eyes narrowed slightly.

I continued to smile.

Brent jerked his head at my bag, grabbing our attention. "What do you have in that duffle that's so important?"

That was easy. "A picture of a kiss. It'll be big news and money to the papers."

Grigori stiffened. "Someone tried this over the kiss between Zoya and me?"

I nodded. "Having breaking news in a world that thrives off the newest information is nothing new. It's not the first time I've been hurt after getting the story first. It's just a hazard of my job. I normally scope out the competing press that's in attendance when I'm on assignment, but I haven't had the time to do it yet. I don't know who the diehards are compared to the diehard crazies."

"Sloppy. Your research should have been your first priority," Daniil reprimanded coolly.

I did not look at him but I nodded. Because yes, I should have. Instead, I had gotten wasted and had sex with the Russian mafia boss man.

My priorities had been a little off their mark.

"Ember was correct. We'll do this pro-bono for you," Stash murmured calmly, his smile creepy on his pretty face. "It could be fun."

"There's plenty of water to be had around here. He could be seeing the bottom of the ocean within the hour," Kirill stated evenly. "You wouldn't have to worry about him again."

I tried not to gape. They were all fucking loony.

In the silence of the restaurant, they waited patiently for my answer, as if I was seriously going to say yes. The lyrics to "Amazing Grace" by Judy Collins started blaring. I jumped, banging the ice harder against my cheek as everyone peered to the right.

"What the fuck is that?" Roman asked.

I cleared my throat and started moving toward the sound. "It's my dad calling." He had set the ringtone himself, seeming amused that he knew how to do it.

Zane started choking again.

I finally found my purse under the table after my dad called a second time. I was still on my knees when I answered, "Hello?"

Dad spoke quickly, "Finally! Look, your mother and I need to speak…"

"Dad, I'm a little busy right now," I interrupted. I could finally hear the sirens as the police made their way here. "Can I call you back?"

He was quiet for a moment, then asked stated gruffly, "You sound upset. You haven't been digging for trouble, have you?" I could hear my mother in the background fussing after he said that.

"No, Dad. No trouble. I'm just in the middle of something."

"Well, call me when you're through. Your mother and I want you to meet someone. We swear he isn't anything like the last young man. You actually have a lot in common."

I leaned my forehead against the table. "Dad, I told you no more blind dates." The sirens were almost here. "I'll call you later. Bye."

"Call me back." he instructed quickly.

I hung up, sighing as I placed my phone in my purse. I shoved my duffle and purse over my shoulder as I stood, placing the bag of ice back against my cheek. I stopped and groaned in exasperation. "What is it with you people and staring?" They were all watching me. Silently. They weren't at all remorseful for their blatant eavesdropping.

Ember's shoulders shook. "What type of men does the preacher set you up with?"

A flashback of my last date hit me. "Some are all right and some not so all right." I blinked, coming back to myself. "We should open the doors. The cops are almost here."

CHAPTER 5

Two days after the incident at the restaurant, I was still trying to come up with the perfect twenty-five questions for the interview with Ember. I had not had a lot of time to compile the list, thanks to the investigation at the restaurant, the cops nabbing a new rookie reporter from the Red Buick, me pressing charges against him and the druggie, getting two stitches next to my temple, and still having to cover the charity events.

The word 'exhausted' did not even begin to cover how bone weary I was.

Now I was at yet another party. Instead of dancing and drinks, Mrs. Donovan had been creative, and made three mini-obstacle courses on the first three holes of the golf course here at the resort that were open to everyone. It was a hit because many of the donators acted like they had an itch to get physical after watching all the fights; however, I was not too thrilled. My editor had chewed me out when I had told him I was not interested in joining…now I was.

But, honestly, I probably would have anyway. There were all kinds of gossip and news worthy information zinging by my ears, making me grateful that I had a great memory since I could not fit a recorder anywhere on my tank top and shorts. Only the memory card from my camera was cut into the fabric of the underside of my bra, since I did not dare leave it anywhere unattended. I had done my best to cover the hickie with make-up, but half of my face was a shade of pea green so the added color to my neck was not such a big deal.

I waited with the masses to find out who would be teamed up with whom. The competitors were mixed with the donators and press, and there would be ten teams of ten. 'Awards' were going to be given out to the first, second, and third place teams of this event. I was a little hopeful that I would be put on a team that did place, because more than likely whatever was in those award bags I could sell and have enough rent for three months. Or even a few new pairs of shoes and handbags. Either way, I wanted one.

From a huge cowboy hat, Mrs. Donovan started pulling slips of paper on which the contestants had written their names. The people that were not joining the festivities drank and mingled on the sidelines. I fingered the tiny bandage that covered my stitches as she read names off. I had taken some ibuprofen. It did not currently hurt, but it was starting to itch, the healing process annoying.

A third of the way through the name-calling, I heard her say mine over the portable mike and speaker she was using. I made my way through the crowd, some of them taking notice of me for the first time, putting the face to the name. As they stared, some were hostile, those who I had done unflattering stories on it the past and some were respectful; those individuals knowing it was hard work being a reporter.

Bluntly, I was not loved by all or hated by all. It was hit or miss.

I exited through the front of the masses, and waved at Mrs. Donovan, showing her I was here. Her stare was stony, one of my haters, and nodded to the right. I smiled amiably, and strolled to stand next to three individuals that were starting the third team of which I was now a part of. I almost grinned, seeing a bag in my hand when I saw that Stash was one of the three. I had learned today during his lone obstacle course that he was one fast son-a-bitch. I did not recognize the other two. They looked like donators, since they weren't wearing a competitor's shirt.

I damn near knew we were going to win when Ember's name was called next; she had almost beaten Stash's time today. I did not hear the next name called. But when he came out of the line, I was immediately on guard. Ben Summers walked toward my group, staring directly at me. He was one of my haters. I had done a piece on him that had gotten him thrown out of the big leagues. He was a baseball player—at least, formerly—that I had exposed to doing steroids. Repeatedly.

He most definitely had a grudge against me when he walked past me, slamming his shoulder against my body. Grunting, I fell hard on my ass, barely moving my hand before he stepped on it. I rolled, maneuvering out his way before he decided to *accidently* hit me again. I jumped to my feet, rubbed my ass, and moved closer to Stash and Ember. We had not exactly become friends, but they did not hate me like Ben did. They had also saved my ass once this week.

"Friend of yours?" Ember asked quietly.

"Something like that," I muttered, pulling grass off my shorts.

Stash grinned. "You make friends easily, don't you?"

I shrugged, flicking another piece of grass. "Territory of the job."

Ember cocked her head. "Why do you do it if everyone hates you?"

"People deserve to know the truth. If their hero is a drug user," I jerked my head Ben's way, "then they should know, and pick a new hero."

Stash chuckled, shaking his head. "A truth seeker."

"Any reporter, who's worth their grain in salt, is a truth seeker. That's where the good stories lead you, since the best stories come from the biggest lies," I explained, listening for the next name. I really did have a lot of haters out there. Ben was not the worst.

The next two were competitors with a purple and red shirt.

I rolled my shoulders. Only two more to go. Maybe it would not be that bad.

Then I groaned, hearing the next name. "Shit."

"What? Who is she?" Ember asked, her eyes roaming the mass.

I mumbled, "Chrissy Tumas is a very nasty woman." I had once done a story on her and her wealth, but unknown to me; I had also been fucking her current boyfriend. I had met him on her estate, and I thought he was working there. I had gone on a few dates with the man, and then slept with him during our three-week long 'relationship'. "You know how I said I hate fighting?"

Stash and Ember nodded.

"Well, I have gotten into one fight before." I cleared my throat and nodded toward the woman headed our way, already staring daggers at me. "It was with her."

"Really," Stash drawled, scanning her person. "She's a lot bigger than you. Why did you get into a fight with the heiress?" Ah. He knew who she was.

"I know she's big. She kicked my ass." I sighed. "We fought because she caught me in bed with her boyfriend." I held up my hands when they both looked at me in shock. "Erase whatever is going through your mind right now. The guy was a liar. I also thought he was my boyfriend."

I sighed and stepped forward, and stopped being a pussy. Whatever she did to me was not their fight. Not that I was going to get into a fight. But this was mine to deal with.

"Hello, slut," Chrissy snapped. "Screw any other taken men lately?"

No. Just a man that liked to hurt people for a living. "Hello, Chrissy. I wish I could say it's lovely to see you again, but it's not." I grinned, feeling evil. "How's your boyfriend? Wait. I'm sorry. You married him, didn't you?" Vaguely, I heard Mrs. Donovan speaking again, but I could not hear what she said over Chrissy's hissing. "Does he still do that thing," I crooked my finger back and forth, "with his tongue?" She was such a bitch. In our past, she had broken my arm when she had stormed into that room, not even waiting to talk it through and figure out what the hell was going on.

I could hear Stash and Ember snorting and chuckling behind me.

Chrissy's cheeks turned bright red. "You fucking bitch!" She threw a punch.

I ducked. The shot going over my head, I pivoted away, grinning at her, not able to stop the words. "Oh, wait. That's right. You wouldn't know because he mentioned he hated doing it to his girlfriend before me. She didn't shower regularly." He had once told me this. I tapped my nose, and then pointed at her. "You."

She growled, and charged.

I could not move fast enough.

We went down in a tangle of punching fists and hair yanking.

I saw flashes erupting, and knew my parents were going to give me hell for this, but I hated this woman. While she screamed in my face, trying to slap me, I pushed on the ground, rolling, and slamming her down onto her back.

"You broke my fucking arm, bitch," I hissed, slamming my fist against her face, making sure I did it just like Daniil had to my assailant. *Eye for an eye.* I felt her nose snap under my knuckles, and it was extraordinary and oddly satisfying. She and I were now even.

An arm was suddenly around my waist, lifting me up into the air and away from the now screaming Chrissy. As I hung against whoever held me off the ground, my back against their chest, I learned she knew some very imaginative curses for a spoiled heiress.

Stash was picking Chrissy up, and she lunged at me again, even with blood running down her face, but Stash yanked the bitch back. She pointed, bellowing, "Fuck you, slut. I'll break your arm like I did last time." She kept struggling and shouting obscenities.

Security was storming up behind them.

I stilled completely, making sure I did not look like I was going to fight anymore. I did not want to be taken away. She could not press charges since there were so many witnesses to her attacking first. It had probably just looked like I was defending myself. She, on the other hand…I grinned, brushing my hair back from my face as I dangled in the air. I could actually press charges if I wanted to.

I would not do that though. I had gotten my eye for an eye.

Mrs. Donovan and the Mayor reached us before the security did, and Mrs. Donovan rushed to me, stating, "I'm so sorry, Ms. Forter. We'll have her removed immediately."

I bit my cheek so I did not smirk. "Thank you. And you can calm down. I won't put my viewpoint in an article. Your charity won't be hurt from my writing."

I saw relief flash over her beautiful features before she nodded and snapped her fingers at the security officers, herding them to the bleeding, belligerent Chrissy, who Stash was still dealing with.

The Mayor stood in front of me. "Are you injured? Do you still want to compete?"

I nodded, the back of my head rubbing against a hard chest. "I want to compete. I'm fine. I want one of those award bags." I tilted my head forward, and whispered, "Can you tell me if there's any jewelry in them?" I loved me some sparklies. I had never had them growing up, so when I splurged and bought one, I treasured it.

His cold mien cracked for a heartbeat, and I saw amusement in his eyes before they frosted again. "I believe my wife put some in the first place bags."

I grinned. "I guess we'll just have to win then."

The Mayor nodded, his eyes glancing briefly over my head before he left.

Patting the muscular arm that was around my ribs, holding me in an unbreakable grip, I muttered, "You can let me down now. I'm done fighting the wicked bitch." I tilted my head to the side, glancing up.

And froze.

Daniil. It was Daniil. Why my shark radar had not gone off, I did not know. He had been a constant blip on my 'screen' for the past two days. I always made sure to keep a visual on him when I was at the events, keeping him at least in my peripheral. It was best to know where the danger lies. Or stands, in his case.

I sucked in a breath and stayed very still. He had not bothered me since the restaurant, but one of those bodyguards had been following me around everywhere I went. The guard normally did a fabulous job of making himself invisible, but every once in a while I caught a glimpse of him, Least Ugly. With the guard still following me, it had to mean that Daniil had not calmed down from his earlier threat.

I stared into his face as he watched me, his hair hanging down against his cheeks. The tiki lamps that were lit made his hair shimmer like the dark night sky above us. His expression was bored, but his eyes hid something that I could not see because of the darkness. I wet my lips, and slowly whispered, "Can you let me down, please?"

He breathed in; his chest expanded against my back. "That was a nice punch."

I blinked. "It should have been familiar. I picked it up from you the other day."

He stared. "Did she really break your arm before?"

I nodded slowly. This was an odd conversation. Crazy. "Yes. A year ago."

He jerked his head toward Ben, who was watching us. "What about the first idiot that hit you? What's the story there?"

I cleared my throat, and was not quite sure what to do with my arms since he still had a hold of me. I ended up just letting them dangle. "I ran a story about him using while he played professional baseball. He blames me for his career's demise."

He stared, still. "Hmm…"

I blinked, and muttered again, "Think you can let me down now?"

Guess not. He did not move, instead asking, "How many enemies do you have here?"

I was exasperated. Mrs. Donovan, the Mayor, security, and Chrissy were going to be leaving the area soon. He and I were going to become noticeable shortly. "Honestly? Too many to count." His eyebrows lowered, which I ignored to pat his arm. "Now. Please."

Instant. "Did you run that search on the other reporters?"

"Yes. No other whack jobs here." *Other than you.*

I squirmed, reminding him I was still physically in his hold.

"You haven't been wearing your glasses," he stated, watching me struggle.

I banged the side of my head against his chest. "I put in two week contacts the day I had a hangover. No reason to waste them."

He stated coolly, "You look better without them. They're horrid."

"Yes, you've already said that before."

"It bears repeating," he spoke softly…right before he dropped me, just as everyone started to move out from in front of us, the masses now back in view.

I stumbled and quickly caught my balance, rubbing my ribs under my breasts. I would probably have a bruise. Moving promptly through the last of the security team, I stood next to Stash, asking him quietly, "Why is Daniil over here?"

He shrugged. "He's part of our team." *Shit.* He grinned. "For someone who hates violence, that was one hell of a hit."

Ember chuckled. "Don't forget about her mom. Anti-gun coalition." She peered across Stash to me. "You do realize that will probably be in the papers with all the photos that were taken." Her chuckle deepened. "Ironic, that."

I groaned. "Yeah, my parents are going to love it." I heard the name Mrs. Donovan called out to fill Chrissy's place. "Are you shitting me? She has to be doing this on purpose!"

Stash asked dryly, "Don't tell me, another friend?"

"He wants to be," I muttered, tilting behind Stash. "He's my own celebrity stalker."

"A reporter with a stalker." Ember laughed outright. "That's fucking ironic too." She glanced at me. "You're just full of ironies, aren't you?"

"Not by choice," I answered, watching as Samuel Packard came out from the crowd.

Ember whistled low. "Tell me why you're not friends with him? He's gorgeous."

"Yeah, until he calls you twenty times a day, sends you flowers at least once a day and leaves you little notes on your apartment door in the evening and the morning." I shook my head. "I wouldn't screw him if my life depended on it."

Samuel was ten feet away and heading straight toward me when I felt heat on my left side where the cool night air used to be. I glanced over, and I mean, what the fuck kind of evening was I having because Daniil was standing right next to me and staring at me with a confused and disgusted mien just about the time that Samuel arrived directly in front of me.

"Hello, Beth," Samuel said quietly, smiling down at me, using a pet name that he had no right to use. "You look beautiful tonight."

I stated dryly, "Samuel, my face is half green. I have dirt and grass stains all over me. My hair looks like I stuck my finger in a light socket. I'm in no way beautiful right now."

He placed two fingers on my bruised cheek, and whispered intimately, "You look as gorgeous as you did the first night here when you couldn't decide between the red dress and the black one."

I froze. Same as Stash, Ember, and Daniil. *How the hell...*

"Did you invite him into your room before the ball?" Daniil asked casually.

"No," I hissed, disgusted beyond belief.

Snap. Snap.

Honestly, I was not even sure how Daniil did it. One second, I felt like I wanted to puke because Samuel was still touching me. The next second, I saw a flash of Daniil's hand right before Samuel was shouting and holding his two twisted, broken fingers.

Stash chuckled as Samuel ran away. "Next!"

I dug through my first place bag, sitting on the grass in the midst of the Lion Security's group where I had tagged along since there were so many 'unfriendlies' in the crowd now that they all knew my face. I was a sweating, dirty, disgusting mess, but when I felt a small velvet box, I did not care if I was bone weary. I grinned, yanked it out, and popped the lid. The tiki fires provided enough light to illuminate a pair of heart shaped ruby earrings.

My heart deflated as I fingered my decidedly holeless earlobes. I had never gotten them pierced, and

I did not plan to. I did not want any holes in my body that were not already there.

I mean, it could have been a ring or a brooch. Not everyone mutilated his or her body.

I sighed and grumpily snapped the lid shut. At least I would have grocery money for a few months if I got a decent price out of them at the pawnshop or on eBay. I tossed the box back into my bag, and started rifling through it again.

"Not what you were wanting?" Daniil's voice drifted from above me.

I froze, and then slowly turned, looking up from my seated position. He had disappeared after we had completed the obstacle course. I thought he might be going to bed…since he was…older. Instead, he appeared even dirtier than when he had left.

He sat between Zane and I, making us scoot unless we wanted to be squashed.

I watched him warily as I resituated myself. "No. My ears aren't pierced." I swallowed, and turned back to my bag, being a very bad reporter and not even listening to everyone else's conversations. Because the bag was so full, I started pulling each item out. I concentrated on each piece, firmly ignoring the man next to me. I started estimating the price I could get for each item that I did not want, keeping track on my fingers how many hundreds it was.

I was at seven hundred when Daniil asked, "What are you doing?"

I stopped and pushed the items aside that I had

gone through so far, feeling a little braver as he was not moving to kill me. I tried not to smirk when I said, "I'm sitting."

He chuckled softly. "Cute, Ms. Forter. But what are you keeping track on your fingers?"

I turned my head and stared. He was rich. He would not understand. I pointed at the items. "I'm trying to figure out how much I can get for all of these if I sell them. So far, I'm at seven hundred bucks. I like to buy nice things and live in a nice apartment, but that takes budgeting." I turned my attention back to the items before he could react. I did not want to see him laugh at me. Hearing it would be enough as it was.

There was not a chance to hear anything like that when Zane asked loudly to their group, "Who wants play cards and drink beer?"

An uproar of shouts sounded.

I leaned forward, around Daniil, and told Zane quietly, "The resort's alcohol shipment was lost. Evidently, that restaurant wasn't the only place. All the businesses around here use the same distribution center, so they're all bone dry."

Zane stared. "Who told you that? And when?"

"The bar here at the resort, and I double checked with the front desk. I found out the same night as that guy attacked me. They said they would put up notices when they have more in. The only stuff left is non-alcoholic beers or virgin drinks." I shook my head. "Have you ever had a non-alcoholic beer? It's like watered-down piss."

Zane blinked. "Oh. Well. That does suck." He cleared his throat, standing like everyone else. "Good night, Ms. Forter."

I waved my hand, putting my items in my bag. "Call me Elizabeth." He was all right unless he felt like you were threatening his friends. I was not planning to threaten any of them. Daniil had scared me off that, so much so, that I still had not decided if I was going to keep investigating the Grigori/Ember possible affair. I was very much on the fence with that subject, and trying to find a way to drag the Donovan's name through the mud without it, but I was not sure it could be done. "And good night. Happy winnings."

Zane chuckled. "Oh, I'll win." He thumped Lev's shoulder, asking him, "Does a three-of-a-kind beat a straight?"

Lev snorted. "Yes." He removed Zane's hand and left.

While I gawked, Zane grinned. "See." He was still smirking like the winning fool he was going to be as he walked away.

I glanced around the golf course, realizing Daniil and I were the only ones still seated from their group. There were still other groups sitting around talking and enjoying the cooling evening, but that was not enough for me. I quickly shoved the rest of the items in the bag and jumped to my feet. Daniil easily followed, staying next to me, not moving away.

"What are you doing?" I asked, slightly mystified.

He ran his fingers through his hair, and his lips

twitched. "I'm standing, Ms. Forter." His eyes roamed down my body, and his nose crinkled.

I was confused as hell and more than a little irritated. Not a great combination. "I know I'm no great beauty, but what is it about me that repulses you so badly?"

His eyebrows snapped together, but slowly, and from the sound of it, honestly, he stated, "No. You're wrong. You are beautiful, not the exotic type, more country beautiful. But you're just so small." He waved his hands in a womanly shape, but extra thin, like the hourglass was pint-size. "I've never been attracted to someone who's as little as you. Most of my lovers have," a gesture of an extra-large hourglass, and then he held his hand way up to his lips indicating a tall woman, "more to them. I can't figure out why I find your kewpie-doll face, wild hair, and breakable body stimulating."

I blinked. "Um...thanks?" *Crazy.*

I turned, and began walking away, but I heard him curse softly. My eyebrows came together in confusion as I heard the grass crunch under his feet, and then he was at my side, slashing a hand through the air, stating as we walked, "I'm sorry. That didn't come out right. I'm usually much smoother than this."

"That's great to know," I mumbled. I blinked. I stopped in my tracks; Daniil also halted, as I understood his crazy language. My eyes went wide, and I turned my attention to him. "Are you hitting on me?"

He placed one hand on his hip while running his

other through his hair. He puffed out a breath, and looked me up and down, and again, his nose crinkled. "Yes. Yes, I think I am."

"You think you are?" I muttered, bewildered, but held up a quick hand when he opened his mouth. "Never mind, but I do want to clarify something." I stared, wondering if he understood just how crazy this was and trying to find a way to figure that out. "Just the other morning you threatened to kill me. In many ways. You frightened me worse than I had ever been. You did this after we'd just had sex the night before. Now, you want to have sex again. With me. The one you shouted at, and threatened to strangle, slice, and smother."

His mouth slowly opened. No sound escaped. He blinked.

Ding, ding. About damn time he figured out how insane this was.

I shook my head and started marching away. He was one truly twisted individual. It was obvious that he had not even realized that his actions were wrong the other morning. That had just been him, doing his thing. One of the truly sad parts was that he had acted as though he was doing me a favor as he talked so pathetically about my body, like I would jump the man as soon as he said the words.

Crazy old asshole.

I heard the crunching of grass again, and I sped up. This was getting fucking ridiculous. I had gone from being scared shitless of him—I still kind of was—to trying to outrun an interested suitor. I had no idea how the fuck this had happened.

"I'm not interested, Daniil," I said over my shoulder, seeing him gaining. I scowled at his muscular legs. They were fucking long. I peered back where I was walking and quickened my pace even more. "I'm sure you can find someone else to fill your bed."

"Yes, I can," he stated factually, his voice too close.

Confident, crazy old asshole.

He gripped one of my elbows from behind, jerking me around to face him. I winced as he crushed my arm. He quickly released me, scowling when I instantly started rubbing it. "You're so fucking bitty."

"You. Already. Said. That!" I exclaimed, throwing my hands in the air, grateful that we had made our way to a clearing where no one was. "I'm small. I'm short. My tits are smallish average." I pointed in the air, clarifying. "Though, I have a nice ass." I pointed at my head. "I have crazy hair. My face reminds you of a doll." I waved my hands up and down my frame. "And yes, my body is definitely breakable compared to yours. We have covered all of this. Now leave me alone."

I turned to leave, and he jerked me back in place, much more gently this time. "We aren't through." He kept a grip on my arm even though I repeatedly tried pulling it away. "I need to say something so quit running from me."

I gritted my teeth and breathed deeply. "Speak."
Then leave me the hell alone.

He dropped my arm and glared. "I'm not a damn dog."

I scowled right back, crossing my arms. Waiting.

He began pacing, muttering, "You're very aggravating." His eyes darted to me. "I'm only going to say this once, so listen closely." I waited, drumming my fingers against my arm in irritation. "You're a reporter, one who has it out for my son's company and the person, people, he loves. I couldn't tell you a damn thing about the circumstances that are happening here. And I still won't. I'm not sorry for what I said that morning. The timing could have been better though."

I eyed him as he stopped pacing. It just bubbled out. "You're crazy."

He looked exasperated. "I told you to listen closely." His head tilted. "And yes, I am a little crazy. Most women find it an attractive attribute."

Only the cracked would say that.

He stared.

I started to turn; until I realized he had said something before that last bit. He had said 'listen closely'. I halted with one foot turned away, goody-bag dangling from my crossed arms.

What had he said?

I stared at the grass that was evergreen in color, only lit by the moon.

My excellent memory began replaying his words.

I was a reporter.

I had it out in 'general' for Grigori's company... and the person he loves.

Circumstances going on here.

He would not take his words back.

Read between the lines. Listen closely.

He had threatened me because his son loved Ember, and he would do anything to protect his son, and Ember evidently, which included scaring, not actually harming me because I was the big bad reporter that had it out for them.

My God.

I stood stumped for a full minute until a thought occurred, and I turned back to face him where he stood silently, watching me. "What would you do if I ran an article stating that Grigori and Ember were having a love affair behind Brent's and Cole's backs?"

He rubbed his chest, staring at the sky, the moon kissing his face, making him look like death's angel. Slowly, he stated, "I would demand a retraction because it's not true." *Right now.* He did not say the words, but I heard them nonetheless.

"What if it became true?" I asked slowly. "What would you do then?"

"I would buy the first paper and frame it," he murmured softly. "As long as the timing was right."

I stared hard. "What if I had talked about what I heard that morning?"

He shook his head. "I take care of my lovers. I made sure you didn't talk."

I understood what he was saying, but still… "You're crazy."

He shrugged. "It works for me."

I let my arms dangle by my sides. "When were you first interested in me?" I was still confused as hell.

"The first day when you bumped into me you smelled like roses. I wasn't sure who you were at first, but you looked familiar. From your tiny picture in the paper, I later realized. I asked Stash. When I pointed you out to him, that's when we saw you slip under the bleachers. I was furious then. And if I'm going to be honest, it helped because I was a little confused by my attraction to you."

I blinked, and mumbled stupidly, "You smelled like roses, too. It's the resorts soap and shampoo." He did not say anything, and I cleared by throat, the dumb cobweb disappearing. "Why did you come into the bar that night?"

"To question you; I wanted to know what you were investigating." He cocked his head forward, his hair hanging around his face as he eyed me. "Why do you want to run a story about Ember cheating on Brent and Cole?"

I smiled a little. "You have your secrets. I have mine." I paused, and decided to be a bit honest. "I don't have it out for Grigori and Ember. They're just a means to an end."

He stiffened, growling, "They're no one's means to an end. I won't allow them to be."

I was quiet for a few moments, and then shook my head, saying softly, "And we were doing so well, too." I pointed at myself. "I'm a reporter and I'm being honest. Everyone is a means to an end to some story." I sighed and kept up with the truth. "Daniil, from what I can remember, the sex was great between us, but this," I pointed at him, then me, "isn't going to happen again. You're not exactly the type to sit back and let me do my job if it's not what you want to run in the papers. I don't let anyone get in the way of the truth. If I had actual proof that Ember had poisoned Zoya, I wouldn't have done the article myself because you scared the shit out of me. But I would have sent it on to someone else to run, if he or she wished. No one should have the right to stop the truth from being printed."

I paused. "Well, unless it's a matter of national security. That, I understand. But you…you would try to stop me on everyday stories, and probably, in a scary as hell way." He had taken a few steps forward, closing the distance between us. I stood still. I did not think he was going to hurt me for what I had just said, but his size was an intimidating factor. "There's also the problem that you don't want your kids knowing you're having sex. And truthfully, no offense, I'm not sure how comfortable I am having sex with someone who's a helluva lot closer to my father's age than my own." Staring up at him this close in the dark, he looked even more like death's angel.

He bent his head, and whispered, "All of what you said is true. I would try to stop you from writing an article that's not conducive to the plan. I'm not positive I would frighten you again. I would probably just bribe someone, or scare that person from printing it. And no, I definitely don't want my kids knowing I'm having sex because they seem skittish by the fact that I have a sex drive after their mother's passing. And truthfully, no offense, I'm not sure either if I'm entirely comfortable having sex with someone your age. I've always kept my lovers above my children's ages." His head tilted farther, and his hair brushed the side of my face.

He watched as my breath caught. "We were both drunk before. It couldn't possibly have been as good as we both remember. Perhaps we should let a kiss decide. If it's as good as we remember, maybe we can work around those other details." His voice was a low purr, his accent deepening. "If not, there's no harm in trying."

Embarrassingly, I was panting. My heart pounded because I did remember how good it had been to kiss him. I licked my lips, staring at his. "I guess one kiss wouldn't hurt."

"Exactly," he murmured and slowly lowered his head even further.

I dropped my goody-bag and placed my hands on his shoulders, running my palms around his neck to hold him just as his hands landed softly on my hips, pulling me against his warm body.

That's when our lips touched.

And...I learned...being drunk had dulled the senses.

His lips were the fireworks and mine were the fuse. It was as if an explosion rocked us as we pressed our lips harder against one another's. I gasped and altered my hands, gripping his hair as hard as his arms were that slid around me, crushing me against his body. We groaned at the same time, and his full, soft lips opened and his warm tongue instantly met mine. The explosions rocked us again for an unknown amount of time, and we went a little crazy as our tongues tangled and caressed one another's with a carnal hunger I had never felt before.

I could not breathe. I really did not care. But I started to get dizzy and yanked my head back…and it slammed against something hard. "*Oomph!*" Blinking blurrily, I stared at Daniil's face.

His eyes snapped open wide, glancing left and right. "Shit."

I wiggled, realizing I had something against my back. One of my legs was lifted over one of Daniil's hips as he held my thigh; his other hand fisted in my inhuman curls. I gently extracted my fingernails from his rock-hard biceps and peered at our surroundings with him. We had somehow moved, at least, ten feet from where my goody-bag lay in the grass. My backside was currently pressed against a palm tree.

Holy shit.

Slowly, I turned my head to face Daniil.

He was staring at me. Like a shark. A death angel with shark eyes.

He wanted to take me down under in the most sinful, carnal way.

Somewhere, Dad was screaming a prayer, because I was drowning. More than willing.

"Ignore them," Daniil muttered, breathless, his tongue sliding back across mine.

I went dizzy with it, but I jerked my head back. "I can't. They're just…there." His bodyguards were a wall in front of the elevator doors as we went up to his room. Their backs were to us, but they were in the damn elevator as we made out behind them.

He growled, pushing my back against the wall, taking my mouth again.

And holy hell, it was like the ambrosia of fireworks.

I groaned and yanked on his hair, pulling him closer.

He rumbled again into my mouth, lifting me off the ground.

Wrapping my legs around his waist, I ground against his erection.

He moaned deep and pressed against me, pushing his cock harder against my core.

I whimpered. I wanted him in me now. Like… *right now.*

"Sir?" Ugly Duckling asked loudly.

We both jerked at the sound.

Yeah, it was easy to ignore them with his lips on mine, and his cock against my clit.

I tilted my head, looking behind Daniil, even as he turned to glance over his shoulder.

We both stared for a second.

I squeaked.

Daniil cursed.

His three guards, Least Ugly back on duty with his boss man, were standing outside the elevator with Ugly Duckling holding the door open. The elevator was making a vulgar buzzing sound, which meant he had been holding it open for a while. The worst part was that Zane and Stash were standing right next to them ogling us. Over the buzzing sound, I could hear others of Lion Security out in the hallway, talking about whose room was biggest to play cards in.

My jaw was gaping, but I stared at Zane's hand and pointed. "Is that a Coors Light?"

It was a brown, long neck bottle with a silver label.

Zane made a gurgling sound in his throat.

Grigori's voice sounded not too far away. "What's wrong with the elevator?" He paused, and then asked quickly, "Is Papa in there?"

I sucked in a harsh breath.

Daniil jerked us across the elevator, pressing me against another wall.

Swatting Ugly Duckling's hand from the door, he then hit the button for my floor.

I hissed, "My award bag!"

Least Ugly had it in his hand. Ugly Duckling had Daniil's bag.

It would be obvious if they had two. Plus, I wanted it, dammit.

"Shit!" Daniil arched back, with me clinging to him, and snatched it.

Hopefully, no one noticed out there.

Zane was outright laughing now. Stash was still standing dumbstruck, his jaw hanging.

Daniil pressed me back against the wall and started pounding on the button to close the door. Daniil zeroed in on Zane, hissing, "Cut him off!" The doors weren't closing very fast after being held open so long.

Zane was not going to be of any help though, because he was almost doubled over, but Stash blinked and moved to the right. Immediately, I heard Stash start speaking to Grigori, which meant he had almost been on us.

Daniil whispered to his bodyguards, "Her room." The doors shut.

Both of us stared at the closed doors. Breathless.

I started giggling.

Even though that had been embarrassing as hell, it was also funnier than shit.

Daniil turned his head to face me. "That was not funny." His lips twitched.

I gurgled. "Stash looked like he was going to faint."

Slowly, he lowered me to the ground. He started chuckling. "I haven't had to sneak around with a woman since I was a teenager. It appears I'm a little rusty."

I laughed harder, holding up a hand. "I don't need the reminder of how long ago that was for you."

He growled, grabbing the back of my neck. "Enough with the old man jokes. I'm minutes away from showing you just how old I'm not."

I wiped my eyes. "Then don't use words like 'rusty'." I snorted.

Instantly, I was being twirled. He slammed my back against his chest...and he bit down over the hickie on my neck. I stilled, and my breath caught as he held me immobile. Shivering from the intimate dominance, I slowly whispered, "Fine. You haven't called me little girl or teased me about my age since that first day. I won't do it to you either."

He nodded slightly, his teeth still gripping my skin, and then he leisurely licked over his mark. "I think our time together will go a lot smoother without any added problems. We have enough as it is." He stood upright when the elevator dinged and the doors opened.

Walking down the hallway to my room, I asked, "So are we just doing this while we're here, or are we going to extend this after we get back to New York?"

Staring down at me, his eyes heating as they roamed over my body, and again his nose crinkled. "I don't know."

I lifted a hand and rubbed a finger over the top

of his straight, perfect nose. "Quit doing that. You're going to give me a complex."

"What?"

I crinkled my nose. "This."

He stared. "I didn't even realize I was."

"I get that you don't understand why you're attracted to me, but," I waved my widespread hand in front of his face, stopping in front of my door, "quit showing it so much."

He chuckled and grabbed my keycard from my hand. Wrapping me in his other arm, he pressed me against his chest so quickly his chuckle ebbed away. Staring down at me, his eyes fired with desire. His voice was a low timber as he rumbled, "I think I can manage that."

CHAPTER 6

Yanking him down to my mouth, I pressed my lips to his. I nipped his luscious bottom lip, and a rumble sounded inside his chest as he opened the door behind my back, banging my goody-bag against the wood as he kissed me back. I stumbled backward into my room, pulling him with me. Standing in the entry, he pressed his tongue inside my mouth and ate at my lips, slamming the door shut and dropping my goody-bag.

Gripping his shirt, I pulled it up his chest and ripped it over his head. I left the lights on in my room so I could see all his beautiful muscular flesh. I slapped my hands down on his pecs, and he lifted me, my legs draping around his waist immediately.

"Where's the bed?" he asked quickly, his voice deep, and then took my mouth in a carnal kiss even as he tugged my shirt up, only breaking away to yank it off me.

"Regular room. Just around the corner," I mumbled, licking over his lips as my hands ran over his heated skin that was smudged with dirt from our first place win.

He growled and wrapped his arms around me, crushing me against him and pressing his mouth hard against mine as he walked, bumping into the closet area and bathroom. I groaned, quickly becoming addicted to him sliding his tongue over mine, rubbing it like his cock was going to do to my core. Flicking my bra, he unclipped it and yanked it off me, never separating from my mouth. I was panting and groaning, and felt him bump against my bed. On his knees, he climbed onto it blindly, his hands running down my back. He let us fall the rest of the way, catching some of his weight on his elbows, his face moving to my neck.

That was when I felt the bed shake.

Not from us.

A scream worthy of a thousand deaths sounded in my ear.

My heart stopped for the barest second, and then I was screaming and gripping Daniil.

Daniil instantly rolled us straight off the bed… with a gun in his hand.

He landed on his back—with me on top of him.

My own shout cut off with a grunt from the impact while he pointed his gun up.

I stared down at him; my fingernails imbedded into his shoulders.

Ever so calmly, he puckered his lips…and blew.

A stray curl of my hair lifted and caught in the rest of its inhuman mess.

Apparently, it had been in his line of vision as he stared up at the bed.

Time ticked for a few moments.

I trembled as he held me with his free hand, wondering who the hell was in my room.

Daniil blinked slowly. His lips twitched. "Ember? Is that you?"

My breath caught in the silence.

A feminine reply from up on my bed, "Mm-hm."

Ember was in my room?

"I would know that scream anywhere." Daniil lowered his gun. "Anyone else here?"

Silence, then… "No."

"What are you doing in here?" he asked as his hand rubbed up and down my bare back.

We both heard the deep, shaky sigh from above, and then she said quietly, "I came in to get my interview done, but," she groaned, "I fell asleep. Christ, I'm so sorry."

I let my head fall on Daniil's shoulder, muttering, "There's no privacy in life."

I heard a choked snort from above. "Full of ironies."

Sighing, I crawled backward, shy when it came to nudity unless the person in my bed was supposed to be there. Daniil's eyes were glued to my bare breasts, and he licked his lips, his gaze turning shark hungry in an instant. I ignored him the best I could, pushing out from between the bed and the wall, and still on my hands and knees, looked for my shirt.

Though my gaze snagged on my luggage and duffle. They were open and had been rifled through. My eyes narrowed, and I breathed deeply. Ember had come in search and had lay in wait for me to return to probably intimidate me or talk me into giving her the damn photo when she could not find it. Not for the interview as she had said.

Finding my shirt, I slipped it on and stood as Daniil sat up from the floor, but he did not get up. I glanced down and saw why. He was rock hard and it showed blatantly under his soft mesh shorts. I found his shirt and threw it to him, jerking my head to the bathroom. "Why don't you go take a shower? This won't take long."

I was pissed. Embarrassment was not even a factor right now. Daniil was staring at me. I could feel it, but I was too busy glaring at Ember to look his way. She was sitting cross-legged on my bed; her cheeks slightly pinked, but she was gazing right back at me with remote eyes.

In the corner of my vision, I saw him sluggishly put the shirt on over his head, and he said coolly, "I wouldn't mind hearing the interview."

My teeth clenched as my gaze snapped to him. Of course, he would not mind hearing it, so he could fucking proofread it and try to edit it. I asked furiously, "Maybe you would just prefer to leave entirely?"

His eyes narrowed, and he got up slowly, pulling his shirt down enough to cover his erection. He opened his mouth, and my nostrils flared, knowing he was going to say something to ruin this before it even began. He stared, and then his mouth snapped shut. He brushed past me and stalked into the bathroom, slamming the door hard enough to shake the walls. A few seconds later, I heard the spray of the shower.

I did not have time to think about what that meant though, because I turned my attention to Ember, who was staring at the wall where the bathroom was with a shocked expression. Picking up my duffle, I threw it at her. "What the fuck do you think you're doing going through my shit? I should report you to the police right now!"

She caught it easily even though she had not been looking at me, and sat it calmly on the bed. "I want the photo."

"I never would have guessed," I shouted, pointing at my door. "Now get the fuck out of my room. If you ever pull this again, I will report you to the cops."

Bristling even more as she leaned back on the bed, getting comfortable, she stated evenly, "If you give me that photo right now, I'll give your father's church a two hundred thousand dollar donation." She reached into her purse on the bed and pulled out what looked like a money order. "I had this prepared if I couldn't find the photo." She neatly placed the money order on my bed.

My mouth shut, my temper instantly gone as I stared at that check with so many zeroes.

"I did a search on you and your family," she

stated bluntly. "Under the donations section on your father's website, it states that the roof needs repairs and the pews need to be replaced." She tapped the money order. "This would more than pay for the repairs needed."

I gulped.

My father had been stressed the previous week after church service. Donations had been down for so long with the continuing recession that everything in the church was starting to break. The church needed that cash. I was not a perfect Christian by any stretch of the imagination, but I could not picture my father's church shutting down because of lack of funds.

I cleared my throat and blinked up at her. I could see victory already in her eyes. It did not thrill me. She somehow knew I could be bought in this manner. I stiffened, coming back to myself now I was not looking at the church's salvation.

I crossed my arms and leaned back against the dresser. "That money order, plus three off the record questions of my choice, right now, for a copy of the photo and a guarantee from you that you won't give it to anyone else to publish before I do." I paused thoughtfully. "And you can't get pissed at me because of the photo and try to back out of our deal for your interview." I was still planning to get that interview with her. It was pay dirt material.

Her eyebrows snapped together. "Why would I get upset about the photo? It does show them kissing, doesn't it?"

I shrugged. "Yes, the photo shows them kissing."

Her nostrils flared like mine had earlier, and she stayed quiet, watching. At least a couple minutes passed as she stared me down. I just waited patiently, thinking about what article I was going to write tonight and get it sent off before deadline, which was coming up...I glanced at my watch...pretty damn quickly.

"Fine," she muttered. "You have a deal."

I nodded, but did not move to get the memory card, asking my first question I wanted to know. "Question one." I saw her shoulders tense, which told me she was wary, planning to tell me the truth. "Have you and Grigori ever been lovers?" Daniil had said, kind of, that Grigori loved her, but that did not mean she'd had sex with him. It could be unrequited love, and if that was the case, I was barking up the wrong tree in my effort to drag the Donovans in the mud.

Ember froze. Her gaze hooded even as her eyes went frigid. That pretty much gave me my answer right there. But 'pretty much' was not fact. "Why do you want to know?"

I shook my head. "Your responding with a question wasn't part of the deal." I waited.

She eventually dropped her gaze, staring at the bedspread, not moving. I finally got my damn answer when she stated, "Yes." She was so stiff she looked like she was going to break.

I sucked in a breath and rested more firmly against the dresser, and took my own turn to stare at the bedspread. Its green embroidered tropical flowers blurred as I tried to decide what question to ask now. I had not been sure before. It had all depended on what her answer might have been, since I had several routes to take. And really, big stories often came from people following their heart or the money. I knew she already had money, even after she gave all of Brent and Cole's worldly possessions back to them when they returned. She had been rich from her late-grandmother, her late-father, and her late-husband. I tried not to stress over the fact there were a lot of 'lates' in there.

My next question was just a nicety before I asked my final one. "Why do you want the photo so badly?" It did not make sense, since it was of Grigori kissing someone else.

Her lips pursed, surprising me when she hesitated. She growled under her breath and then cracked her neck both ways. "You will not print anything about this to harm Grigori." Her eyes were sharp on mine, assessing.

"I already said it's off the record." But boy, my curiosity was now thrumming.

She snorted but answered swiftly. "I didn't trust Zoya, so I sent someone to Russia to dig up what they could on her. She's hiding the fact from Grigori that she's married. I plan to send the photo to her husband. He needs to take her ass back to Russia."

Oh. My. God. I really wished I could print that.

Longing for that missed story, I hopped up on the dresser and got comfortable, leaning back against the wall. I looked her straight in the eyes, asking evenly,

"Are you more in love with Brent and Cole or Grigori?" She had to have loved Brent and Cole at one point. She'd had their kids.

The barest flinch. But I saw it. She barked, "What the hell type of question is that?"

I just stared. We had already gone over what she was allowed.

Ember jumped off the bed, and I scooted back, worried now she was going to kick my ass since she was so furious. She did not come after me though. She just started pacing. She walked back and forth across my room, her body stiff for a full minute before...*shit*... tears started rolling down her cheeks.

I was a bitch when it came to my job, and this was going to be part of it. I had seen many people cry and beg when they did not want me to publish a story. I had never faltered in revealing the truth. However, even my heart ached a little seeing the obvious pain that she hid behind her cold mask, her hot tears spilling down her cheeks as she continued her trek across my room and back.

She suddenly stopped, and when she spoke, her voice was void of any emotion. "I won't ever be in love again."

I was pissed and sorry for her, all at the same time. She had finagled a way around the question and still answered it to what she truly thought. That much was apparent on her face.

Dammit!

I looked away from her. I was so annoyed that my

one question had been wasted...that it took me a moment to realize that she had in essence still given me my answer. It was the fact that she had taken so long to answer. My gut had been right once again.

I nodded and jumped off the dresser, grabbing my bra that was lying on the floor by the bed. I had transferred the photo onto this memory card and erased the rest from my other. Lifting my laptop from my duffle, I pulled the memory card out and quickly made a copy for her on a spare memory stick. Stuffing the original memory card back into my bra, I handed over the memory stick.

She had been peering over my shoulder when I transferred it, and I had heard her quick intake of breath when she had seen the photo. She knew what she had looked like on it, and she had immediately moved away from me, her eyes livid as she stared, but she had kept quiet and stuck with the deal.

But now, within just a moment of time, I found myself flat on my back from my legs being kicked out from under me and a deadly Ember with a forearm to my throat as I wheezed. She stated calmly and slowly, "I'm not going to go back on our deal. However, I am going to tell you that if you tell a soul," she paused, glancing at the bathroom, "any soul about what you gave me or the answers I gave you, I will find a way to make your life a living hell. I can make it happen." She smiled. It was scary as fuck. "Or I'll just kill you if I get bored with the game."

I rasped in a breath, unable to move at all, my eyes wide as I saw true death in her eyes.

She was just as crazy as Daniil could be.

Why the hell did I keep underestimating these people?

Get the story, and get out. Easy enough, and yet I kept fucking it up.

The bathroom door opened, and Daniil stepped out wearing only a towel around his waist, his wet hair slicked back to show his face in stark relief, and water dripping down his bare tan chest and calves. Ember froze on top of me, staring down into my eyes that were bulging as she pressed harder, making sure her threat got through. Daniil rested a shoulder against the wall, asking calmly, "Ember, is there a reason why you're choking Ms. Forter? I somehow doubt that could be good for your article."

My eyes started to water, and I really started to struggle when I felt dizziness take hold.

I had seriously underestimated them both.

He was just going to let me die here on the floor.

But when Ember did not move immediately, still staring at me with those emotionless eyes, mine shutting as true darkness seeped in; I felt the floor vibrate under me and heard him shout, "Get the hell off her!" She was suddenly gone, and I heard her grunt right before I was being lifted in damp arms. I started choking, air coming in hard as Daniil held me, yelling at her, "Go get some damn sleep, Ember. You fucking need it."

I blinked at him. My throat burned and felt

crushed as I got in enough air to stop seeing sparkles. I started struggling in his arms. This had been a bad fucking idea. Really bad, obviously. This group brought nothing but trouble.

"Stop moving," he shouted, still glaring off to the side, but when he looked down at me, I must have been showing some, okay, probably a lot of what I was feeling on my face because he cursed, and dammit, held me tighter. He glanced back up; a quick peek showed Ember sprawled against a wall, holding her head. He stated with instant calm, "Ember, you need to leave. And seriously, get some damn sleep. I know you've been roaming the halls until dawn every night. That's not healthy."

"Fucking bodyguards," she grumbled harshly.

I took my first deep breath and gave a hard shove against Daniil's chest.

Daniil grunted, and almost lost his grip on me as I twisted, but he caught me.

I rasped, "Both of you fucking leave. Now." I shoved him again. "I want you both out!"

Ember chuckled, sounding criminal, as she stood. She strolled right past us. "Good luck with her." I heard my door open. "Remember what I said, Elizabeth." My door clicked shut.

I glared at Daniil, ready to cry. I wanted him gone. Good sex or not, he was bad news.

He stared down at me as I struggled, holding me tightly. Grandly, he sighed, and then stated in quiet voice, "You are not at all what I've always gone for."

I choked, and a sob escaped. What a crazy old asshole. Pushing against his chest was doing no good, so I turned my head and bit his shoulder hard, and really started struggling when he almost released me. But he grunted and leaned down to my shoulder and bit me.

I yelped, my teeth unlatching from his skin.

He instantly released his bite.

I grabbed my hurt shoulder, staring. Shocked. He had never hurt me before. It had only been the possibility of it that had scared me. Now that he had, I did not know what to think of it.

He shook his head, walking toward the bathroom. "You bite me, I'll bite you back."

I rubbed my shoulder, gawking as he moved into the bathroom...and stepped directly into the shower, putting us both under the water's spray.

I was fully clothed. He was wearing a towel. I still had my tennis shoes on!

"What the hell are you doing?" I shouted in a rasp, my voice not recovered.

"I'm showering, Ms. Forter." His stared. "I haven't actually done that yet. If you look carefully, I still have dirt in my hair. All I did was wet that towel," he jerked his head at a soaking towel that lay on the bathroom floor with dirt streaks on it, "and wipe off with it, and get my hair wet. I was listening the whole time. Your father's going to be very pleased with that money." When my jaw dropped, he murmured softly, "I wouldn't have let her hurt you. I thought she would get off you when I made my presence known." He shook his head. "She's really…" He sighed heavily. "She needs some damn sleep. She's not doing well right now."

Oh.

As I blinked water out of my eyes, the water was pooling where my body was bent at the stomach and pressed up against his chest. "You're still bad news." That much was true.

He shrugged, easily lifting me up and down with the motion, the pooling water rippling and splashing. "I can't deny that. However, in my defense, when I choose a lover, I take care of that woman. I won't let anyone harm you." His expression turned forbidding. "If they try, they will be dealt with."

I tried not to gawk. "I'm just asking for trouble if I let this happen."

His expression slowly altered into sensual knowing confidence, his eyes spiraling to shark hungry. "The trouble is half the fun. The other half is all in how you get into trouble."

I felt my eyebrows come together. "Tell me you didn't teach your children that."

He chuckled. "I've taught my children many things, but not that. That's all mine."

I nodded. "That explains a lot."

He shoulders shook. "Thank you."

I sighed in exasperation. "I should be running from you right now."

He smiled, and it was a little daunting. "My legs are longer. I would easily catch you."

I pointed a finger right at the tip of his nose. "You don't play fair."

His smile turned wicked. "No, I don't."

Still a little overwhelmed, I swallowed and immediately grimaced. "My throat hurts."

His grinned disappeared, and he set me on my feet right under the spray, my curls instantly plastering to my head. As the water ran over my face, he gently lifted my chin, bending to view the damage. I shut my eyes against the water's onslaught. I felt his fingers probing lightly, and I flinched.

He cursed quietly. "You're going to have a nasty bruise. It's already swelling." He released my chin. "I'll be back in a second."

"All right," I rasped as he got out of the shower. I started stripping down. I tried not to swallow too much as I peeled my clothing off. I tossed the items out onto the tiles, listening to Daniil speak in Russian since he had not shut the door. I quickly rubbed hotel shampoo that smelled like roses into my hair, feeling the dirt and grime wash away down my body. As I scrubbed my scalp and picked through my curls, I heard him step back into the shower.

His hands were suddenly over mine, and he murmured deeply, "Let me do that." I pulled my hands away, and wiped the water out of my eyes as he started running his fingers through my curls, untangling them. "Are you good with us?"

Even though I felt overmatched around him most times, I nodded. "Yeah, I'm good."

A rumble sounded from his throat, and I opened my eyes to see him staring at my breasts. My rosy nipples puckered instantly under his regard, and his hands faltered before they started working through my curls again; his eyes searing as they slowly traveled down my body, landing and staying at the juncture between my thighs. "Red curls on top and below."

"Strawberry blonde," I mumbled, glancing down, dazed from what just his eyes did to me. I did not wax or get one of those silly lines some women got, but I kept them short and trimmed neatly. It was much cooler that way.

He did not seem to hear me as he stared, his gaze traveling back up to my breasts before he licked his full lips. I let my eyes fall below his waist, and the soaking towel he still wore was glued to his front. I blinked, seeing his massive erection in damn fine detail. I had not actually seen him hard while naked; it had been dark in his bedroom, now I was about to.

I quickly ripped the towel off him, startling him from his eye-voyage. He instantly gripped my hair brutally, but I hardly felt it because I was too busy gawking. "Big." That was all I could manage to say. And it was an understatement. No wonder sex had hurt at first. He had the largest cock I had ever seen.

A pained sound came from him, and my eyebrows snapped together as I tore my gaze away to look into his eyes. Honey brown eyes were darting all over my body, and his hands started moving quickly through my hair as he rumbled, "Your throat probably hurts too badly to do anything now, doesn't it?" He was breathing shallowly. Thank God. So was I. He tilted my head back, washing the soap out of my hair.

Eyes closed, I grinned. "If you think what that bitch did to me is going to keep me from enjoying my evening, you're wrong."

His hands tightened in my hair, and I flinched, and instantly, he gentled his hold. "She's not a bitch. She's just going through a few issues right now."

I opened my eyes, glaring at him even as the sight of him turned me on. "She damn near killed me. That's a bitch in my book."

His jaw clenched, and he focused on washing my hair before he sighed. "Ember's probably a topic we should stay away from."

I sighed too. "Agreed." His son loved her, and she loved his son. Daniil loved them both. It was probably best not to call her a bitch, even though I most definitely thought she was, and my bruised necked backed up that opinion.

He picked up the soap, but I took it from him. I explained, "We need to hurry and get clean. I have a deadline I need to make, and taking it slow isn't going to work for me tonight."

He stared, his eyebrows furrowing. "I'm not used to having to work around a woman's schedule." When I only started soaping up because there was nothing I could do about that, he rolled his shoulders, and muttered, "Not exactly what I was expecting."

I shrugged. "I work. I like what I do. I have

deadlines that have to be met." He grabbed the shampoo, still miffed with a clenched jaw, obviously not appreciating a woman of my generation's mindset. As we altered positions for him to be under the spray, I asked, "Is this a deal breaker?" If he seriously had a problem with me saying we had to hurry because of my job, then this would not work.

Silent and dark, he tilted his head back, apparently undecided; his body was beautifully displayed as he washed his hair; the water streamed down his pecs and rippled stomach down to…I licked my lips. God, his cock was beautiful. I stared.

I reacted without even thinking, dropping the soap and lowering to my knees.

I grabbed his cock and immediately wrapped my lips around the crown, sucking.

Oh, God, he was huge and tasted fucking fantastic.

He shouted deep, jarring, and the movement pressed his cock further into my mouth. I moaned, opening my mouth wider and taking more of him in. His hands instantly fisted in my curls, and he groaned long as he pulled back, and then thrust even farther into my mouth.

It was *divine*.

I licked under his head, and he jerked, holding my head more firmly as I slowly loved his cock, hearing him moan, and then shout when I grabbed his balls, massaging them gently.

He panted, "Take more of me."

OBSIDIAN LIQUOR

I hummed, and opened my eyes, staring up at him as I took him as far as I could. He was so massive; my lips did not even reach where my hand was at the base. He stared down and me, and licked his bottom lip, and slowly started thrusting. "Can you take more?"

My eyebrows snapped together. He was bumping my throat as it was.

His dilated dark eyes darted to mine, and then back to what I was doing, and he quickly nodded. "We'll work on that." *What?* "Faster, my sweet."

The term of endearment shocked me, especially because I could understand, his accent thickening. Moaning in pleasure, I sucked hard. He groaned as I pulled back then started running my mouth and tongue up and down his cock faster. His cock was so silky soft on top of all that hardness that I loved the feel of him thrusting into my mouth.

As I began to move faster, I gripped his cock more firmly.

He shouted in Russian, his grip on my hair almost painful as he drove into my mouth once more before jerking back, taking his cock completely out of my mouth. I almost fell against him, not expecting the quick movement, but I was suddenly lifted into his arms.

I yelped, holding him tight around the shoulders.

His mouth was suddenly against mine, eating hungrily at my lips. "Open for me."

I did, his tongue meeting mine.

He stepped out of the shower, holding me tightly

and keeping our lips connected. He grabbed his shorts from the counter, mumbling against my lips, "Condom this time."

I stared in silent demand to hurry, biting his bottom lip and tugging.

He growled, and held me as he stalked to the bed. We landed as we had before, sans Ember this time, and he instantly grabbed my knees and spread them wide. He ground his cock against my core, both of us groaning before he lifted, and his head went between my legs, muttering, "You want fast. I'll give you fast."

I sucked in a breath, and screamed when he slid two fingers into my core that was already wet from sucking him, and his tongue landed on my clit, rubbing up and down. Pushing up on my hands, I lifted and watched as his pink tongue flicked over my clit repeatedly, making me shudder and dig my heels against the mattress and press against him.

His carnal eyes opened and found mine, trapping me as he slid another finger into me, pushing in further and pressing a spot that had my eyes opening wide as I shouted his name. His gaze hooded as he groaned and drove his fingers in and out more quickly, pressing each time just as he sucked and bit the tiniest bit.

My mind was close to igniting in pleasured chaos, and I grabbed a handful of his hair and ground against his talented mouth. My head fell back as I screamed, his attentions stretching me full, also knowing he needed to do this for his cock to fit without it hurting.

"Press…" I panted. "Press again. Do what…you did before."

Oh, he did.

My lower gut already warmed and tightening, the added stimulation was all it took. The throbbing heat curled out and exploded, rushing through me as I jerked against him; my body arched as my mouth opened in a silent scream. My walls contracted, and my body and mind went to heaven on blissful passion, riding waves of intense euphoria.

His mouth went to my core, and he licked and sucked, moaning as I came in his mouth. He lifted before I was completely done, and I heard the sound of the condom wrapper as I fell back onto the bed, my mind still floating and my body shaking.

I was just starting to come down when I felt his fingers spread me, and his cock placed at my core, suddenly driving into me. I arched, shouting as he gripped my hips and pushed farther, my lowering climax stalling. He tilted his hips as my breath caught, and he thrust in hard, pressing right where he had before. He shouted as I screamed and grabbed his biceps. He started with quick, short thrusts, rubbing the head of his cock against that spot.

I shuddered, and fire shot through me again even though I was stretched so full it was painful. The pleasured pain rocked me, and I whimpered as I came again, my mind back in a fog of paradise. He groaned as my walls gripped him, and he pulled back slamming all the way in.

I choked as he dropped over me, grabbing my hands and holding them above my head, his hips pulling back and driving forward with a force that had me opening my legs wide around his hips, all on pure instinct as I floated, wanting more of him.

He kissed my lips gently even as he thrust into me so hard I knew I was going to be walking bowlegged tomorrow. Slowly, I came down, my breath gone, but I kissed him back, feeling him grin against my lips as he murmured, "It is as good as I remember." Then his tongue was inside my mouth, and I tasted myself on him as our tongues coiled around each other, his wet hair brushing my cheeks, covering us in darkness.

Groaning into my mouth and thrusting faster, he reached down and held one of my breasts, squeezing gently and groaning even louder. He felt so damn perfect as he slid in and out of me, and I grabbed the back of his neck with my free hand, sliding my fingers up into his satiny soft hair, holding his mouth against mine.

He asked against my lips, "Am I hurting you? Can I go faster?" His eyes searched mine as his movements faltered below.

Shocked, my eyes went wide. I sputtered, "Faster?"

His eyes lowered, and he shook his head. "It's all right. Never mind." His lips moved against mine again, kissing me again.

But I yanked his head back, stating, "If you can seriously go faster, then prove it."

He froze. "I'm not hurting you?"

I shook my head.

He grinned, and I had never seen this smile before. It was a little devil and a little boyish. Pretty much, it was heart searing adorable. "Thank God. Brace your hands up on the headboard, my sweet."

I blinked and nodded; still staring at his smiling lips, I did as he said. He bent to nibble on my nipples, making me groan and squirm, but he was looping his arms under my knees and pulling them up to my chest, so he had to pull back. He lifted up on his arms, and my legs spread on their own accord, wrapped over his bulging biceps. He murmured, "Press against the headboard, and tell me if I hurt you."

"Okay," I murmured breathlessly, pressing against the headboard just as he started hammering into me so damn fast. I arched, screaming as he shouted, throwing his head back, his muscles straining as he found a rhythm that had me shouting with each deep thrust.

"Fuck, Elizabeth. Shit," he shouted, dropping his head and staring into my eyes, saying something I could not understand because his accent was getting to heavy.

"Can't," I sucked air, "understand you."

"Beautiful," he groaned. "You're fucking beautiful."

I moaned when he tilted his hips, hitting my clit with each thrust. "Beth. Call me Beth."

"Beth, my sweet," he ground against my clit, "come for me again."

Freaked that I had given him permission to call me that, I shook my head. "Can't."

He pressed harder, and I jerked. "Yes, you can." He bent, kissing my lips. "Come for me. I want to feel you come again." Grinding against me, his mouth was heaven on mine.

I whimpered, my hips flexing even more against him. I shivered and ordered, "Harder."

He grinned, and pressed his pelvis against me and rocked back and forth.

I stilled. Screamed. My hips went wild against him, and my hands pressed harder against the headboard. He sucked in a breath, as I felt myself trip…trip…and I fell over the edge, slamming my hips against his. My lids shut, and I felt him kiss me even as he gasped; then he was lifting up and repeatedly hammering into me. I moaned; my head long past gone into sensual overload as an orgasm from ecstasy took me. I could not think. Nothing but the pulses of passion and Daniil's wild thrusts were all I knew. I was pretty sure I heard him shouting in Russian; I drifted in a place I had never been before.

His thrusts became chaotic, and suddenly, he slammed into me, sliding over my cervix and lodging his cock so damn deep. My eyes fluttered opened, blinking out the haze and coming down from my own paradise. I saw him staring down at me; his jaw clenched tightly as his eyelids drooped, and he shuddered, jerking against me hard, lodging even farther into me, his cock beginning to pulse inside me.

He groaned low, his body shaking, and instinctively, I caught him when he started to drop on top of me. His orgasm racked his body, and I felt him come for what felt like forever, my core extremely sensitive after my third orgasm, so I felt every single pulse, making my own body jerk. His hands crept under my ass, and he held us tightly connected until he sucked in a breath, his taunt body going sated and limp over me. I was good with that since mine had done the same.

The air conditioner in my room kicked on, and since our bodies were covered with a light sprinkle of sweat, I felt instant relief from the heat. As I sucked air, our chests heaved against one another's. My hands were on his back from catching and holding him through his orgasm, and I left them there as he moved one of his hands up to the small of my back, holding me. I was not positive how long we lay there; his large body sprawled over mine, covering me, and oddly, I did not mind the shallow breathing.

We both dozed off, because when there was pounding on my door, we both jerked at the sound. Daniil's head snapped up; he blinked down at me sleepily. A fucking gun was in his hand he must have hidden in his shorts that lay next to us, along with his wallet and an empty condom wrapper.

That woke me up fast, and I kept my gaze off it as the pounding sounded again. Since no one was shouting 'fire', I asked in irritation, "You brought a damn gun into bed with us?"

His head had darted in the direction of the door that could not be seen from where we lay. "You know who I am. I always have one with me." He paused. "Get used to it." A blatant command.

Instant. "No. It's not something a woman just gets used to. And don't think that because we had good sex you can order me around."

I saw his eyes narrow, and still not looking at me, he asked coolly, "*Good* sex?"

I pointed against the nose that was facing away from me. "Fine. Fantastic, mind-fucking-blowing sex. But that doesn't give you the right to order me around."

His eyes were still narrowed, and he opened his mouth, but both of us stilled when we heard Zane shout from out in the hallway, "Open the fucking door!" More pounding. "Unless you want me to come in!"

"We better get that," I grumbled, miffed at Daniil and his gun command.

"You aren't going anywhere naked," Daniil ordered bluntly, pulling back, and very gently sliding out of me.

I froze, still very sensitive, but managed to demand, "Quit ordering me around!"

He growled, glaring, but quickly removed the condom and stated gruffly, "We're going exclusive. I don't want anyone seeing you naked but me. Do you understand now?"

I blinked, sitting up slowly and carefully since—oh, yeah baby—I was sore. "You're supposed to ask if I want that. Not just tell me."

He paused, getting off the bed, even as Zane started shouting again outside. He was not facing me, but when he spoke, it sounded like he was trying for patience and speaking through clenched teeth. "Do you want to be exclusive, Beth?" Then he muttered under his breath, *"They normally fucking beg me for it."*

"I heard that," I stated dryly, but really, I was more than a little shocked because when he used my nickname, it reminded me that I had actually given him permission to do so. I cleared my throat, thinking. I had given him permission, which meant something. He would be more than enough for me. I also was not positive after this experience that I would want to share him either while we did this. "Is this just sex?" I had to know.

He paused, his shoulders stiff. "Do you want it to be more?"

My lips thinned. "I don't normally do exclusive unless it's a real relationship." I scratched my head, still thinking. Finally, I added quietly, "I wouldn't mind trying something past sex with you." He was trouble, but he was the delicious darkness that you slipped into freely.

He stared at the wall, silent for a long moment. "We would need to keep this between us for a while. My children…aren't ready for news like this if it's not somewhat serious."

I understood that. My decision was set. "Okay. I'm game if you are. We're exclusive."

He glanced back at me, nodded once, and then bent and gave me a quick peck on the lips before straightening. He shouted over the increasing pounding, "Zane, just a second."

The hammering stopped, and we both heard him shout, "Fucking finally! Hurry up!"

I slipped off the bed, tossed the condom wrapper away, and got my robe off the chair at the small table by the window, slipping it on as Daniil put his shorts back on after disposing of the condom. I got to the door first, and opened it, only to have Zane brush past me quickly, bumping me against the wall. "Hello to you, too."

"Whatever." He walked farther into the room, and I shut the door, seeing Daniil's bodyguards outside my room, standing against the far wall.

Zane glanced at me as I followed before looking back at Daniil, who was sitting on the bed that had obviously been used for sex with the comforter like it was. Hell, Daniil was even in disarray; his hair had dried and it was an adorable mess all over his head, and he just looked...well...sated, relaxed, and leaning back on the bed. I did not even want to know what my hair looked like if his thick, gorgeous straight hair looked like that. I put a hand to my hair at the same moment Zane glanced at me again. He had opened his mouth to say something, but his gaze went to where my hand was, and he kind of blinked at my hair. Jesus. It had to be bad. I went to my bag and started digging through it for a hair tie. It was just long enough that I could get it pulled back if I needed to.

Zane cleared his throat, still staring at my hair, and started speaking in Russian. Quick Russian from the sound of it as I found my hair tie. I was not even surprised, really, that he was doing that. I was a reporter, and he would not have come to my room when he knew what Daniil and I were doing without a damn good reason.

I yanked my hair back the best I could. It really was ugly up because it was not long, but it was better than the alternative. Once I had it fixed, I turned to face them. I stopped in my tracks. Daniil had frozen on the bed and was listening to Zane avidly. Something big had happened. Really big by the way Daniil said something, also in Russian, and when Zane replied, he jumped off the mattress, grabbed his wallet and went directly to the bathroom and got the rest of his clothes. He sat back on the bed and continued to speak to Zane, their conversation picking up in speed as he quickly put his socks and shoes on.

He jumped up again, pulled his shirt on over his head, his gorgeous muscles rippling with the movement. He stalked in my direction, quickly stating in English, "I've got to go."

I was holding my tongue so badly, but I could not help it. Being a reporter was too deeply imbedded. "What's happened?" I was practically bouncing on the balls on my feet.

He shook his head. "I can't say, but I promise to tell you tomorrow if it's true."

My lips thinned, but I could tell he was not going to say more. I nodded. "All right." I would just have to sneak out after he left and try to figure it out by myself.

His lips twitched, and then he leaned down and gave my lips a quick caress. "Don't forget about your deadline."

My eyes snapped to the clock. "Dammit!" I did not have time to sneak out. I would probably be late as it was with my article. I scowled, and he looked like he was trying hard not to laugh. I pointed at the tip of his nose. "You better tell me tomorrow."

He took my finger and kissed the tip of it, chuckling. "Only if it's the truth. That's all you talk about, anyway."

Grumpily, I took my finger back and crossed my arms. "You better go. Zane's looking exasperated." And a little amused. At me. Asshole.

My door burst open, and Daniil and Zane instantly had a gun each pointed at the entry.

It was only Stash who stopped right inside the door with a keycard in his hand.

His hair…well…it could have given mine a run for its money in inhumanness right now.

Daniil and Zane casually lowered their weapons.

I smacked Daniil's arm, seriously getting irritated with the constant gun show. "How many times a day do you bring that thing out? You're going to end up shooting someone!"

Stash's mouth was opened to say something, but they all stopped. Stared at me.

"What?" It was true. The statistics were undeniable about people accidently firing a weapon that it was bound to happen with how many times he brought the damn thing out.

Daniil's lips were twitching again.

Zane murmured dryly, "Elizabeth, that's kind of the point." He raised his gun to the wall behind the bed. "You lift." He peered down the gun. "You aim." He jerked his hand. "You fire." He lowered his gun. "Hopefully, shooting them before they shoot you."

I put a finger to my temple since it was starting to throb, and shooed them with my other hand, muttering, "I've had enough of Lion Security today. Go away."

Daniil chuckled, bending and kissing over my bandage at my temple. "Sleep well, Beth."

I nodded, followed behind them with Stash yapping away in Russian. I started to lock the door once they were gone, but there was a gentle knock. I opened it back up and Least Ugly was standing there with his hand extended, which held ibuprofen and a couple of icepacks. He stated, "Mr. Kozar wanted you to have this for your throat."

I took them gratefully, and closed and locked my door, sighing as I grabbed my laptop. I proceeded to write one hell of a fluff piece. By the time I lay down for bed, my eyes would scarcely stay open. Even if I had wanted to go out and investigate what was going on, I would not have been able to do it efficiently. I fell asleep on a pillow that was still damp from Daniil's and my hair. I smelled roses even in my dreams.

Waking up to my ringing phone, I groaned and then winced. My throat hurt worse this morning. I slapped a hand down blindingly on the nightstand and fumbled until I felt my cellphone. Answering it, I mumbled, "Hello?"

"You're supposed to be reporting the news, not starring in it," my editor shouted.

My eyes snapped open, and I glared at the alarm clock seeing it was 6:04 in the morning. "How many articles are running about Chrissy and me?"

He continued yelling, "Every single fucking reporter who's down there wrote about it. With photos." He growled. "All but one reporter that is. Can you explain that to me?"

"It was personal," I muttered. I did not want Chrissy and my history flashed all over the place. It was embarrassing enough just knowing that I had been deceived so badly before.

"Dammit, Elizabeth, we should have been the ones reporting it!" I heard him breathing hard over the line. "Do I need to pull you from there? Are you going to start breaking everyone's noses?"

I snorted, still feeling satisfied. "No. No more fighting for me."

He stated gruffly, "If you pull another stunt like that…first, you had better give me a damn article on it…and second, I'll have to pull you from there. We write about blood, not cause the blood. Hear me, Elizabeth?"

"Yes. I hear you. It won't happen again," I muttered, but I was talking to a dead air because he had already hung up on me.

I dropped my phone next to me and rolled back over. I needed more sleep to deal with this shit today, and my parents were sure to call soon. Closing my eyes, I tried to ignore how badly my throat hurt, and fall back asleep.

My eyes opened when my phone started ringing again. I glared at the alarm clock when I saw that it was only 6:24. Dammit. My parents had always been early risers.

I grabbed my cell and put it to my ear, and since it had not been my dad's ringtone, I immediately answered, "Yes, Mom. I know what you're going to say. Fighting is the gateway to true chaos." I yawned and stretched.

A masculine chuckle sounded in my ear, and I froze. Daniil purred over the line, "True chaos is made by the weak." He paused, and said darkly, "I'm not weak, Beth."

I blinked, and asked, "How did you get this number?" It was a private cell number.

"Childs play, my sweet." He chuckled when I

huffed. "I called to let you know that if you want the breaking news about last evening, you need to be down in the Sands Restaurant by 7:00 for breakfast."

"You're going to tell me?" I asked, sitting up in bed wide-awake.

"I could. Or you could just happen to be in the restaurant before we all go down there, and hear it for yourself from them. What would you prefer? Hearsay or a first person angle?"

First person, of course. I paused. "Why are you doing this?"

He hummed. "Let's just say this story is conducive to the plan."

I paused, thinking it through. "Are you using me?" He had better not be.

He chuckled. "No more than you're using me. I told you last evening I would let you know, and I keep my word." He paused. "I've got to go. See you at breakfast, Beth."

"Okay," I whispered, hanging up. I stared at my phone. A grin slowly lifted my lips.

It really just might work between him and me.

CHAPTER 7

November 14, 2014—The last day of the charity event…

Standing inside Daniil's posh hotel living room, I stared at the memory chip and tape recorder I held. Not moving, I thought hard about each and every time the Donovans had stopped me from printing an article, or making me write a retraction the next day. Painfully…and sadly…I realized each time it had been about protecting their son. None of the stories had ever been anything to cause them jail time or show them as some type of crook. Never. The stories had all been matters of the heart, something that would have only hurt them—and others—if the information had been known. My head started to spin, and I rubbed my temples, feeling the stitches that were going to need to come out soon.

Least Ugly peered down at me.

I sucked in a breath and asked, "Do you know the real reason why I came here?"

He answered, "No. I had wondered. This charity event is small potatoes for you."

I nodded. "I asked specifically to come. I took another report's place." Licking my lips, I stated for the first time in my life, "I came to find a story on the Donovans that could hurt them deeply. Obtain justice for all the times they held me back from telling the truth."

His head cocked. "Did you find what you were looking for?"

I stayed silent for a full minute, reviewing again in my head that this was the right decision. And again, I came up with yes. "I found it." I wiggled the equipment in my hands. "I have it all here ready to write and send. It could be in the papers by the morning."

"Is it criminal activity?"

I shook my head. "No, but it does involve their son Cole. Matters of the heart." The news that I had gained in Sands Restaurant was nice. Ember had broken off her relationship with Brent and Cole. However, it had not been the golden story. What I held in my hands was. "It would hurt him; and with him, his parents in the process."

We were both silent. I stared at the equipment while he watched me.

Finally, I asked quietly, "Do you have a lighter on you?" I now knew that he smoked.

A few ticks went by, and he asked dryly, "Need a cig?"

"No. I need to burn this information. It's too tempting."

He dug into his pocket, handing me a black lighter. "You're going to burn the truth?"

"Yes. This doesn't need to get out. He's hurt enough." I picked up a glass and set it on the coffee table. Tearing of a few sheets of stationery, I wadded up a piece and put it in the bottom of the cup, and pulled the tape from the recorder. I placed it and the memory card in the cup, and then another wadded sheet on top of that. Sucking in a deep breath, I lit it. "I shouldn't have even seen it."

Least Ugly stayed by my side, watching as the paper burned, taking a box of cigarettes out of his pocket and bending to light one by the flames. He inhaled; his eyes were on the melting memory card and tape. "It must have been some pretty deep shit for you to react this way."

I chuckled. It did not sound nice. "Don't even ask. I'm not telling."

He shrugged, saying in a high voice, a definite lie, "I wasn't going to ask." Puffing on his cigarette, he muttered, "I have a feeling that was good reading though."

I chuckled. It definitely would have been. Until my eyes widened. "Oh, shit!"

The fire was getting out of hand, spilling and flicking over onto a sheet of paper.

Ugly Duckling raced across the room, dowsing the ever-growing blaze with his bottle of water he had been sipping on. He gave us both glowering glances, and plucked the cigarette from Least Ugly's mouth and dropped it into the charred cup; it sunk into the standing black water. He stared down his nose at us, coughed once, and then walked stiffly back to the wall he had been standing against, next to the other guard.

Then Daniil's bedroom door banged open and down the hallway stormed a breathless Daniil, sniffing the air heavily. It was bedtime, so he only wore only a pair of black, Calvin Klein lounge pajama bottoms that were loose on the leg and long, hanging halfway over the tops of his bare feet. I noticed that he had a better pedicure than I did. He sucked in air; his large bare pecs rising with the motion and abs constricting, his gaze darted all around the room; each guard suddenly frozen. And, oddly or maybe not for him, the first thing he zeroed in on was the cigarette butt in the blackened cup. His gaze flew to me, hardening, and he took two steps, grabbing my chin and smelling at my mouth.

"I didn't smoke," I explained calmly, since he looked ready to tear someone's head off.

He sniffed in Least Ugly's general direction, where he stood next to me. Least Ugly ground his teeth together when Daniil's hands immediately went to his pockets, stealing his cigarettes—all without taking his eyes off me. He crushed the box in his hands, and turned his attention on him for a second, stating, "Smoking's bad for you, and others."

His mouth flapped until he sputtered, "So I've been told."

Daniil had already turned away, his muscles tight as he chucked the broken box of cigarettes into a trashcan. He glanced down at the charred mess on the coffee table. "Who did this?"

I yawned. "I did." I was getting sleepy.

Zoning in immediately on the glass, the obvious origination point of the fire, he reached out, and with two fingers, he pulled the memory card and tape out. He stared at them for all of a heartbeat before flicking their curled blackened husks on the coffee table, making a little splash in the water. "What was on there?"

"A story; one that I didn't want to be tempted with."

His black brows rose, instantly curious. "What was it?"

"I'm not telling." And I would not.

He assessed me for a long moment before he asked, "How did you obtain the story?"

My lips twitched.

He glowered, turning his sharp regard on Least Ugly. "She snuck away from you again?"

I instantly moved forward, running my hands up his chest. "It wasn't his fault." I shrugged. "I'm just good at sneaking away when I want to."

Daniil growled, glaring a moment longer at Least Ugly, before glancing down at me. His brows puckered adorably. "I don't like it when you do that. He's there for your protection. I have many enemies, Beth."

Yes, he did…and his children weren't exactly

thrilled since Daniil had told them about us last night during a private dinner. "I won't do it again." *Not for a little while.* "Why don't we go to bed? We have a long flight tomorrow." We were headed back to New York City. He was not going back to Russia any time soon, not with his kids' lives a mess like they were. I was learning he was one hell of a loving father, even if he showed it in ways than what I was accustomed to.

He instantly wrapped his arms around my waist. "The bedroom sounds nice."

I could not help the grin that spread across my face. "Nothing will be happening tonight, mister." I stood on tiptoe, whispering against his ear, "I'm on my period."

He blinked. Stared…grunted.

I chuckled quietly. "You can quit paying off the staff here and at every restaurant we go to." When his expression turned innocent, I laughed louder. "Did you really think I wouldn't catch on about the alcohol?" My amused gaze lit on his fierce one. "I'm not pregnant. Quit worrying."

His chest heaved against my hands. "I'd wondered how long it would take you to figure that out." He bent, kissing the tip of my nose, whispering, "I do want you in bed now. I sleep much better with you next to me."

I warmed inside. "You are a hard man to resist."

His brows quirked, teasing, "Does that mean you're ready to tell your parents?"

My lips curved, kissing him softly. "You're not that hard to resist."

My parents were never going to find out. I liked Daniil that damn much.

He chuckled quietly. "Thank God."

About the Author

Scarlett Dawn is drawn to all things quirky and off-beat. She believes there are no boundaries for an imaginative soul. Her love of the written word started at an early age, when her grandmother would take her to bookstores every weekend. Dreams came alive within the books she found there, and now, she is thrilled to share her stories with others who have fallen under the spell of taking fantastical journeys.

Scarlett resides in the Midwest with her family.

Where to Find Scarlett

Facebook.com/AuthorScarlettDawn

Twitter.com/ScarlettDawnUSA

Goodreads.com/author/show/714179
2.Scarlett_Dawn

ScarlettDawn.net

Thank you for taking time
out to read Obsidian
Liquor. To get news and
updates from Scarlett,
subscribe to her newsletter
at
http://eepurl.com/4X1rv

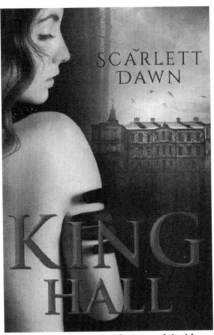

A fresh, meaty, sink-your-teeth-in-and-hold-on-tight new adult fantasy series kicks off with King Hall...

King Hall — where the Mysticals go to learn their craft, get their degrees, and transition into adulthood. And where four new Rulers will rise and meet their destinies. Lily Ruckler is adept at one thing: survival. Born a Mystical hybrid, her mere existence is forbidden, but her nightmare is only about to start. Fluke, happenstance, and a deep personal loss finds Lily deeply entrenched with those who would destroy her simply for existing — The Mystical Kings. Being named future Queen of the Shifters shoves Lily into the spotlight, making her one of the most visible Mysticals in the world. But with risk comes a certain solace — her burgeoning friendships with the other three Rulers:

a wicked Vampire, a wild-child Mage, and a playboy Elemental. Backed by their faith and trust, Lily begins to relax into her new life.

Then chaos erupts as the fragile peace between Commoners and Mysticals is broken, and suddenly Lily realizes the greatest threat was never from within, and her fear takes on a new name: the Revolution.

THE COLD MARK SAGA

FALL

SCARLETT DAWN

A savagely wicked new adult sci-fi serial blasts off with Fall, the first installment in The Cold Mark Saga...

Only one thousand Humans survived The Travel from the shattered Earth. Some Humans say it was their penance for crushing such beauty. Eighteen-year-old Braita merely thought it was pathetic - pathetic that her people had been that blind.

Now, the Humans live in the solar system, Kline, where three planets are habitable. Joyal, the smallest planet, is embraced by the Humans - their family to love as they had never loved Earth. Though a planet covered mainly in water is dangerous real estate to dwell upon.

Their worry turns into devastating reality when Braita's blessed village is struck by a tsunami. Population numbers must be kept to a minimum. Drastic measures must be taken. Braita's life is twisted in brutality when she is chosen as one of the three hundred Humans to be removed from Joyal...and sent to the Mian, the aliens to fear, on the planet Triaz.

Thrown head first into a barbaric world she knows nothing of, Braita must adapt to a dark life as a slave of the Mian society. Her existence depends on it...and possibly, the fall of her heart.

Made in the USA
Lexington, KY
22 November 2015